Historic China
Spandrell

West Martian Limited Company
1st Edition, March 2025

Content from *Bloody Shovel* is property of Spandrell, and is used with permission by West Martian Limited Company.

First printing 2025

The publisher can be contacted at westmartian.com

ISBN-13: 979-8-3492-1968-9 Paperback

Table of Contents

- Emotion 9
- Choices 13
- The Bow of the King of Chu .. 19
- Tales from the patriarchy 24
- Patriarchal Sexual Law 30
- The Water Margin 39
  - Male culture 41
  - The Law 51

Proverbs...............................61

Stuff White People do...........63
Socialism qua Entropy watch 72
On Attrition........................77
The purpose of absurdity......80
Giving the handle................86
Names................................92
Correct Naming..................95

The Song...............................99

The Song Golden Age........101
The distribution of power....109
The Song Dynasty's Decline 115
The Song Dynasty's Fall......120
The Song Dynasty's Surrender
.....................................128

The Great Ming Emperor Admonishes his Troops about Women 142

The 36 Stratagems 147

There's always a way 149
The Honeypot 153
The Empty Fortress 158
Sow Distrust, and Profit 162
The Self Harming Trick 173

Bureaucracy & Monarchy 175

The Chinese Bureaucracy, 1 177
Chinese Bureaucracy, 2 187
Chinese Monarchy 195
Chinese Monarchy, 2 202

6 - Historic China

Historic China

8 - Historic China

Emotion

2015-06-10

One of the things that strike when reading Chinese history is how everybody cries a lot. Not women; prime ministers, army generals, high officials are crying all the time. This is often used in historical shows to add dramatic flare.

When you ask people why is everybody crying, the answer tends to be "oh, they got emotional". Emotion. What does that mean? It always struck me how this outbursts of emotion always happen when it's convenient. See how all those Mandarins cry in front of the Emperor. Well that's all they can do to express their will if the Emperor isn't buying their arguments.

Think of a typical interaction. Emperor wants X, Mandarin doesn't want X for whatever reason. Maybe he thinks it's insane, and will bring disorder; or he think it will affect him personally and he doesn't like that.

So:

Emperor: I want X.

Mandarin: X is not a wise idea your majesty.

10 - Historic China

E: Shut up, I want X.

M: But your majesty, Confucius said blablablablanonXblablabla

E: Fuck that, I want X.

M: I brought 20 famous ministers to say that X is bad.

E: OK I'm getting pissed now, X or else.

What do you do now? Well you can accept defeat. Or you can cry. Fall to the ground and cry your eyes out.

M: Your majesty!! For the sake of the Sages of old, of the rules of your ancestors!! Please!!!

Now the point of crying, or "emotion" in general, is that it's an involuntary bodily reaction, which signals that the person is so affected that usual brain operation doesn't work anymore. It's a way of calling attention to an emergency. This is serious stuff your majesty. I'm crying, you see.

For some reason outbursts of emotion are taken as some expression of a better, truer self. The brain is the rational, self-interested, scheming part, so when emotion takes over that's by definition your not scheming, self-less, godly heart speaking.

But that's crap, of course. Emotion is done in the brain. So by definition it's computation. Your brain takes some inputs, analyzes them, and makes some output to further some purpose of yours. Sometimes the output says: Your majesty, X is not a wise idea. Some others, your brain judges that your purposes are better served by falling to the ground and crying our eyes out, while squeaking like a girl. Surely Emperors known to be merciful to weak people were more likely have people cry, while Emperors known for hating crybabies and flaying them alive didn't have many mandarins cry at them.

This works of course for all other sorts of emotion. Anger only happens when anger is advantageous. See how everybody today soon gets filled with righteous anger at people who dare oppose gaymarriage, while 10 years ago nobody did. Opponents of gaymarriage are weaker now than 10 years ago, so being angry at them is advantageous. You get more of what you reward.

Same with offense taking. Offense used to be[1] what rich aristocrats took when their reputation was questioned. Daring to suggest that a rich merchant was a crook made him really really offended, the more offended the more accurate the accusations. Also mere contact with low status commoners could make a high status person livid with offense. Today, offense is what women and protected ethnic groups feel when a white man dares say anything

---

[1] https://intellectual-detox.com/2015/03/23/standing-up-to-offense-bullying/

about them. Microaggressions are felt because they are profitable for the microagressed.

Different emotional reactions depend on their perceived potential results, and that depends on the power relations. If you're weak, you're better off crying. If you're strong, you're better off getting angry. It doesn't mean you're faking it. Simply that everything happens for a reason. That includes your anger, your sadness, your happiness, and everything else you feel, especially when you express it to others.

Choices

2016-02-04

I hadn't thought about it, but my last post on Whites converting to Islam has a somewhat similar theme to a very famous episode in Chinese history. It's been a while since I write another Chinese history tale, and this is one of my favorites. So let's talk about Wu Sangui 吳三桂.

The year is 1644. The Ming Dynasty is in ruins. It is actually in ruins; a peasant rebellion led by a man called Li Zicheng 李自成 has been ravishing the country for a decade, conquering and utterly destroying much of the central and western areas of the country. The rebel leader had already conquered the largest city in the west, Xi'an 西安, and had proclaimed himself as the king of the Shun 順 Dynasty. The Shun army raced from Xi'An up through the province of Shanxi 山西, where most of the cities openly surrendered to him without bloodshed. In no time he crossed the western passes close to Beijing, and on May 26, the capital fell. The emperor of the Ming Dynasty stabbed his wives and daughters with his own hand, and then hanged himself on a nearby hill.

A resistance had formed in the south, where several imperial princes were proclaimed as emperors in different provinces. The north though was completely in control of the rebels of the Shun Dynasty. They felt safe, and spent 10 days sacking Beijing, raping the wives and daughters of the mandarins and merchants, and torturing them to extort untold quantities of gold and silver. Then one advisor to the rebel army came with news: we haven't completely conquered the north. There is still Wu Sangui.

Most maps you can see of the Ming Dynasty are complete bullshit, because they throw in every place where the Ming ever had a garrison during its 270 years of life. And this guys had lots of garrisons around at first, but they soon abandoned most of them. For all purposes, the effective northern borders of the Ming Dynasty were the Great Wall, which they built.

By this time, May 1644, mostly everything south of the wall and north of Yang-tze river has fallen to the Shun rebels, and most Ming generals in the area had surrendered and joined the fun. All except the most important. You'll see in this map that there's a weird discontinuous piece of wall up in the Northeast. That's Liaodong 遼東. That used to be firm Ming territory, settled with Han farmers, but since the 1600s a nearby tribal people, the Manchus (Jurchens back then) had built a very strong state, and conquered most of the Ming settlements in the area. The Manchus were extremely good fighters, they had managed to beat the Mongols and put them in their army, and had been raiding inside China for decades, doing massive damage. By 1644 there was only one fortress left in Liaodong, the castle of Ningyuan 寧遠. And Wu Sangui was its commander.

Weeks before Beijing fell to the rebels, the Ming emperor had sent an edict to Wu Sangui, ordering him to abandon the fortress and come with his troops to defend the capital. He was actually on his way, not far from Beijing, when the city fell and the emperor killed himself. Unsure what to do, Wu Sangui got his army and moved back to the Northeast, and set camp at Shanhaiguan 山海關, the last fortress of the continuous Great Wall, where the wall meets the sea. The fortress was very strong, and he decided to hold up there.

Soon the rebels having fun at Beijing decided that all Ming generals had surrendered, surely this one would surrender too. What is he going to do, fight us? The conquerors of the capital? Good luck with that. The rebels soon found that Wu Sangui's family was all in Beijing, 38 persons in all, led by his father, who had been chief of the capital's garrison at the time. They... persuaded the man to write a letter to his son, saying how virtuous and sagely the rebels were, that the game was over, and his duty as a filial son was to obey and surrender to the rebels. He'll be given a title of nobility and treated with all the honor he deserves.

The letter gets to the fortress, alongside shitloads of gold and silver for his soldiers. Wu Sangui sees that this is a pretty good deal, gets his army and marches towards

Beijing in order to formally surrender to his new lord. On his second journey to Beijing in a few days, he suddenly bumps into two servants of his household. "What are you doing here?"

-Oh you have no idea, young lord.

What happened? How is my father?

They got him, my lord.

Who got him? What happened to him?

One rebel general came to father, and asked him for your concubine, Chen Yuan. Your father refused, said she wasn't there, that she was with you, but they refused to believe, and they tortured him. They tortured all of us, it was awful, only we two were able to escape. Father Lord was tortured so badly that he's likely to be dead by now. You should prepare yourself, young master.

Not good. Not good at all. These rebel bastards were scamming him. They didn't want him to surrender and join their army as a general. No, they wanted to lure him to the capital to kill him and get rid of a problem. That they didn't wait to steal my women and torture my father is proof that nothing good expected him at Beijing. Oh, this won't do. Wu Sangui again got his army and led them back to the Great Wall fortress.

What could he do, though. His army was perhaps the best in the empire. Tough, hardly men from the Northeast frontier, seasoned by constant war with the fierce Manchus. He had a sizable army, but could he beat the rebels? All of them? Soon he heard that Li Zicheng, the rebel emperor himself was personally leading a 100k strong army to kill him. And behind his back, on the other side of the Great Wall, Dorgon, the effective king of the Manchus had departed from their capital with two thirds of the fierce Manchu army. He obviously knew that his Chinese enemies had collapsed and he wanted part of the fun.

So there he is, our famed general, holding the strongest fortress on the Chinese empire, facing a 100,000 rebel army on his front, and another 100,000 army of Manchu riders on his back. What can he do now? The Manchus are on his back. His uncle are with them; he was captured years ago, and had surrendered to the Manchus. He was now a very high status nobleman in the Manchu state, and he sent letters to his nephew to surrender. These are good people too, manly, virtuous, just men, not like the corrupt and decadent mandarins who used to rule over us. You cannot trust them, nephew. They maybe Chinese like you and us, share our culture and language. But they are evil, false men, and you know that. Join the Manchu army, they know of you, admire your martial skills, they'll make you into a prince and give you untold riches and honor.

The rebel leader though has brought Wu Sangui's father with him. He tells him it has all been a misunderstanding. One of the top rebel generals got a bit carried away. But the Shun emperor guarantees his safety, and he seems to mean it. He calls him to fulfill his duty towards his father and his country. The Mandate of Heaven has changed, the Shun now has it. His duty as a general is to follow him, and start a new glorious dynasty. Once the old corrupt mandarins of the Ming Dynasty are dealt with, the new, vigorous armies of the Chinese nation will come back north, where he can take part on the glorious retaking of the Northeast from the evil barbarians. Do the right thing, general. Your family and your nation need you.

Guess what he did?[2] 2 days later his father alongside the 38 members of his family were killed. 2 days later he was made a prince. The Manchus ruled China until 1911.

---

[2] https://www.amazon.com/Great-Enterprise-Reconstruction-Imperial-Seventeenth-Century/dp/0520235185/

The Bow of the King of Chu

2016-05-21

Google openly praises leftist terrorist supporters, Obama forces schools across the US to allow transexuals to choose the toilets they use. The West is fucked up. Yes, I know. The mission of this blog has been to explain in plain language why the Left exists, why it's so crazy, and why it gets even crazier over time.

Part of that mission is to find similar instances of crazy political ideas in non-Western cultures. Sir John Glubb spent some time in the Arab world, and he seemed to have the same interests, so he produced a very interesting account[3] on political madness in the Abassid empire, which looked fairly similar to contemporary leftism. I live in East Asia, and so I write a lot about East Asian history. I may end up making some money by selling my readers a fancy book with some stories. In the meanwhile, let me share another interesting anecdote.

The most fertile era of Chinese intellectual culture coincided with what came to be called the Axial Age. In

---

[3] https://www.isegoria.net/2014/07/the-effects-of-intellectualism/

20 - Historic China

China is the era between 550 BC and 200 BC, more or less. That's the era of the Hundred Schools of thought. China was divided in many kingdoms, who each wanted a piece of each other. It was if anything more violent and chaotic that Classical Greece, which had similar dynamics; division, constant warfare, and amazing intellectual life.

This is of course the era of Confucius, Laozi, Sunzi and all that. Some of you may have some general idea about classical Chinese thinkers, but it's also important to understand what was going on there. What kind of intellectual climate existed in that time. What happens when everyone is coming up with new ideas all the time? Think about it in contemporary terms. What happens when everybody and his grandma has his own ideas is... a whole lot of signaling spirals. See a small example. There was an old story about a king of Chu

聞楚王張繁弱之弓，載忘歸之矢，以射蛟兕於雲夢之圃，而喪其弓。左右請求之。王曰：'止。楚人遺弓，楚人得之，又何求乎？'

A King of Chu was out in the country on a hunting trip. He had a world famous bow, and the best arrows in the realm. So he was out there hunting dragons and rhinos (real story), when he dropped his bow. Lost it. The precious bow! His retinue was looking for it like crazy, but then the King told them to stop. "Stop looking for it. A Man of Chu lost his bow. A Man of Chu will find it. No need to search for it."

To European ears this sounds like a pretty awesome king. A great loving king who cares about his subjects. He lost his precious, world famous bow. But it doesn't matter, because he lost it in his territory. One of his subjects will find it, and use it for the good of his country. King or subject, we are all men of Chu, so who cares? What a great King. The stuff of legend.

The story soon became a cause of commentary across the other kingdoms in China. Every single one of the Hundred Schools had to publish their official stand on this story. What do you think of the King of Chu and his lost bow? It's kinda like modern journalism, where everybody has to rush to publish their stance on every item of the news. Psychologists call this "common knowledge", the social phenomenon where everybody is compelled to comment on something precisely because everybody else is doing so. This creates evolutionary pressures to reduce the total amount of information in society so that everything can be common knowledge and thus become efficient gossip, the fuel of human sociability. But I digress.

A modern nationalist would say that the King of Chu was an awesome king. But what did Confucius say about it?

'楚王仁義而未遂也。亦曰人亡弓，人得之而已，何必楚？'

'The King of Chu is a humane king, but he's still half-way. He could have said "a man lost his bow, a man will find it". Why specify "A man of Chu"?'

The King of Chu wasn't good enough in Confucius eyes because he dared put priority on his subjects, and not be equally nice to all humanity. Because Confucius, of course, was a humanitarian. A universalist. The King of Chu was a petty man who cared about his subjects, not about the entire humanity.

So basically, Confucius today would approve of Angela Merkel and Bryan Caplan. Thanks dude. No wonder he was never taken seriously by any of the dozens of kings of his time, and died a low-class civil servant. His universalism however was catnip for the nascent class of non-aristocratic bureaucrats, who developed it for centuries after his death. They loved this "we are above armies, borders, and that gruesome stuff. We care about righteousness and love, about what is right for all humanity". This in 300 BC. Do you see now why the First Emperor burnt their books and buried the scholars alive after he unified the Empire?

As a bonus, guess what the Daoists had to say about the King's bow.

老聃聞之曰：「去其『人』而可矣。」故老聃則至公矣。

"Why mention people at all?" That's right. A bow was lost. A bow was found. It doesn't need to be a man of Chu. It doesn't need to be a man at all. It can be a snake, or a frog. Or a tree. We are all part of nature, maaan. Want some more weed?

This is explicitly recorded as the Confucians being more 公, more public minded than the King, and the Daoists being more public minded than the Confucians. If this is not a virtue signaling spiral, I don't know what is. And again, this was going on 2200 years ago.

Tales from the patriarchy

2018-02-20

The way of properly learning a language is to do what languages are made for: use it. Ideally, live your usual life, do whatever it is you like doing, and just try to find a way to insert that language you're learning into your daily routine. So if, say, you like movies, and you're learning Persian, well, stop watching Hollywood crap and go pick up some Persian movies.

I get asked about books on Chinese history, and I tend not to know what to say. I haven't read a lot of Chinese history books in English. Certainly not any general ones. I read China in World History by Adshead after Steve Sailer recommended it. It's a fascinating book, not very accurate, but a fun read for beginners, so I do recommend it too. Generally speaking most English books on China are pretty bad, and badly written. With the exception of Frederick Wakeman's, which are awesome.

What I often do to read up on Chinese history is watch a historical TV show, then stop anytime something bugs me and go check out the primary sources out there in Wikisource. If the thing is interesting I check out 知乎, China's much improved version of Quora, where they have detailed explanations and book recommendations. If the topic is interesting enough I get the (Chinese-language) book.

There's a recent TV show in China about 司馬懿 Sima Yi, one of the most important leaders of the Three Kingdoms period. The whole period, which lasted about 100 years, 180 to 280 AD, is the most written about in the history of China, mostly because of the sheer force of personality of the men of the time. Dozens upon dozens of great warriors and statesmen. Sima Yi wasn't the most colorful of them, but arguably he was the guy who won the game. He was a quiet minister of the northern kingdom, Cao Wei, where he served and outlived three emperors. The guy was so good at anything he did, so influential that part of the imperial family decided to get rid of him, lest he took power for himself and made a puppet of the imperial court. He let the court take away all his power for 10 years. Then out of the blue he run a coup d'etat, where... he took power for himself and made a puppet of the imperial court. At 72 year old he executed thousands upon thousands of imperial kinsmen. Then he died. His soon took over, then died. Then his grandson decided to do away with the charade and took the throne for himself. He then started the 晉 Jin Dynasty.)

So anyway, the show is pretty good. But it's of course adapted to modern sensitivities. But not so much, I was very surprised to see a scene where he kills the whole family of his main rival in the coup, 曹爽 Cao Shuang. The usual penalty for treason in China was 夷三族, "leveling of the three families". There are conflicting records on which three families this referred to, but basically it meant killing the whole extended family, clients included. So all wives, brothers, children, parents, uncles and aunts. All beheaded, if possible together. The scene in the series shows Cao Shuang's 3 year old son, tied up in white clothes, in front of the beheading platform. They don't show his head being cut off, of course, but the mere sight of a 3 year old boy in front of a beheading platform would get most housewives in the West calling for their smelling salts and yelling at social media.

Anyway, kudos for China for their accuracy in that front. Shame on China for their lack of accuracy in what remains, in my view, the still biggest and most encroached area of progressive influence in modern China. Women. I write a lot about how Islam is a better deal for Men than Western culture, which is why Muslim immigrants refuse to integrate, and in fact radicalize further in their faith after moving to the West. But if Islam is a good deal, old Chinese culture was the freaking lottery. Polygamy among the gentry in China was not only legal: it was expected. And there was no limit to the number of wives you could acquire. Girls were sold as property at 13-15 years old, and no self-respecting men would not get a new wife every 5-10 years if he could afford to.

Of course having too many wives was frowned upon. It was a sign of lack of seriousness. Women are something men like, but men should like other things more, manly things. Warfare and government. Reading and the arts. Women were entertainment, who also happened to produce children, which are always nice to have, as they make heirs, and daughters which you can give to you friends' sons.

It is unconceivable that a man of the stature of Sima Yi would not have a handful of wives. And indeed he had, four of them in total. His first wife, Lady 張 Zhang, is said to have had a temper. That means that... she had a temper. In the TV show though, tailored to modern sensitivities, for commercial reasons if only, as most TV show viewers are women, Lady Zhang is a kung-fu master who accompanies her mild-mannered husband at war, does ninja work to help him in his conspiracies, and basically runs the household with an iron clit. Amazingly (progress!) the show has Sima Yi welcome a second wife. The show makes it look like the emperor forces upon him a second wife, Lady 柏 Bai to spy on him, and that makes his first wife, Lady Zhang, to flare up in outraged fury. How dare you get a second wife! A good 5 episodes are dedicated to this story. But she eventually accepts the fact and they get along together, the second wife being super smart or something.

Which I guess it's great fun for modern housewives, who like soap operas of women fighting for status. But as a historical show, the whole premise is ridiculous in the extreme. First of all, Lady Bai was his fourth wife. That's 4 women. Second, Lady Zhang was just some boring housewife with a temper, no super ninja. Third, while Chinese wives were indeed never happy about their husbands getting another wife, there was nothing they could do about it. Ancient China didn't recognize divorce, but wives nagging about concubines was one of the few cases where it was granted. Lady Zhang, first wife, may indeed have given shit to Sima Yi about it, but only so much of it, and the idea that Sima Yi would be apologetic about it, that he would feel sorry about getting a younger and hotter wife, is just preposterous.

Don't take my word about it though, the official history of the Jin Dynasty says it for me. The historian in charge was funny enough to add this piece of domestic life of Sima Yi.

其後柏夫人有寵，后罕得進見。帝嘗臥疾，后往省病。帝曰：「老物可憎，何煩出也！」后慚恚不食，將自殺，諸子亦不食。帝驚而致謝，后乃止。帝退而謂人曰：「老物不足惜，慮困我好兒耳！」

Sima Yi spent more time with Lady Bai; Lady Zhang hardly ever saw him anymore. One day, Sima Yi was sick, lying in bad, and Lady Zhang went to see him. Sima Yi saw her and said: "You annoying old thing, why did you bother coming out?". Lady Zhang was so angry and embarrassed that she stopped eating, and was going to kill herself. All her children [note: the elder, most legitimate heirs of him] stopped eating too. Sima Yi was startled and went to apologize, so she stopped (started to eat again). Sima Yi then left and told his men: "the old thing doesn't deserve pity, what bothered me was my poor good boys!".

This anecdote is not only funny today; it was funny even then, as it takes 3 lines of the 8 total lines that Lady Zhang, posthumous empress, got in the official history. I love how he called her, **老物**, "old thing". Plenty to comment here: wives being annoying in any time and any social stratum, wives using their children as weapons in order to get what they want. Human nature.

Sima Yi was a huge prick, unlike the mild gentle man he is in this TV show. In previous renditions he's written more accurately. But hey, he founded a dynasty, he was the towering general and statesman of the most tumultuous and interesting era in 5000 years of China. Of course he was a prick.

Patriarchal Sexual Law

2018-10-29

We live in a world of sexual license. Sexual freedom we could say. You can sleep with whoever you want and neither state authorities, nor most people, will interfere with your sexual life. You can even engage in the most unnatural, disgusting and disease-inducing activities; but criminal law just has nothing against you.

This alone is a sign that the patriarchy doesn't exist anymore. Patriarchies are systems in which all women belong to a man; the husband after marriage, the father before that, or the head of the household if she's a servant of some sort. Women have this uncanny ability to make men want to have sex with them, and at the same time prefer to have exclusivity in that matter. Not to mention the potential for disease or childbirth. So naturally their legal guardians had to take care that women, i.e. their property, was not captured by other men to have sex with them without proper compensation. As such, law regulating sex in the pre-modern period where every bit as complicated, and as harsh, as laws regulating finance and property in our day.

Imperial Chinese law on marriage is a lot of fun, but most interesting are their laws on fornication. Fornication belonged to criminal law, ever since the very first complete legal code on compiled during the early Tang Dynasty in 624, which has remained to us as the 唐律疏義 *tánglü shūyì*. More importantly, rape was understood as fornication + force, a more serious crime but nothing really different. The difference is stark between a legal code which lasted pretty much intact for 1300 years, and our present day of female supremacy, when rape has been reinterpreted every few years as the single most heinous crime that can be committed, while at the same time requiring no standards of proof.

What follows is a translation of the legal code of the Qing dynasty (1644-1911), the 大清律例 *dàqīng lǜlì*, tome 33. I have the book but you can find the text in Wikisource[4].

犯姦 Fornication

> 凡和姦杖八十. Any fornicator gets 80 strokes of the big stick.

杖 *zhang* was a big wooden stick with a flat surface, the worst of two available corporal punishments. It was normally applied to the buttocks or the back. If done strongly it could kill a fit man after 50 strokes or so. The

---

[4] https://zh.wikisource.org/wiki/%E5%A4%A7%E6%B8%85%E5%BE%8B%E4%BE%8B/%E5%88%91%E5%BE%8B#刑律·犯姦

traditional maximum was 200, so it was usually never applied that strongly. Bribes to the executioner in advance helped make him feel weak that day.

At any rate, 80 strokes for peaceful, consensual fornication is a lot of strokes. 80%+ of the sex going on in any modern society is fornication. Think about that.

有夫者杖九十. If there's a husband, 90 strikes.

Obviously any consensual fornication with a woman with a husband is morally worse than if the woman is single, so you get 12% more strikes of the big fat wooden bat.

刁姦者[無夫有夫]杖一百. Seducers get 100 strokes, whether the woman has or does not have a husband.

> **刁姦** supposedly meant getting to fornicate on false pretences; the man (or woman, I guess) getting to seduce the other part by lying about its attractiveness or something. 100 strokes to you for lying. -

強姦者絞. Rapists [literally "forced fornicatiors"] get hanged. Not immediately, most death penalties were done after review on autumn. But rapists got hanged, period.

未成者杖一百流三千里. Attempted (but unfulfilled) rape gets exile to 3,000 li away.

A li was a bit more than 500m during the Qing (set at 576m around 1900), so about 1,700km away. -

凡問強姦須有強暴之狀婦人不能掙脫之情亦須有人知聞及損傷膚體毀裂衣服之屬方坐絞罪 This is commentary to the law: "All cases of rape require proof of violence, and proof that the woman couldn't get away. Also they need someone in the know (i.e. a witness) and damage to the skin [of the victim] as well as her clothes, in order for the penalty of hanging to be valid."

若以強合以和成猶非強也. If intercourse starts as forced but ends as consensual then [it means] it wasn't forced".

Important point here. Very important point. Again this is commentary later added to the law. I wonder what case(s) prompted this to be added.-

如一人強捉一人姦之行姦人問絞強捉問未成流罪""If one man forcibly captures [a woman] and another man rapes her, the rapist gets hanged. Attempted rape gets exile"

又如見婦人與人通姦見者因而用強姦之已係犯姦之婦難以強論依刁姦律 If a man sees a woman fornicating, and because of that rapes her, it's unfair to argue it's rape, and so it's sentenced as "seduction". So rape of a fornicator gets you 100 strokes of the rod, not the death penalty. Hey, she was in the market after all.

姦幼女十二歲以下者雖和同強論. Fornication with a girl below 12 years old gets treated as forcible (rape), i.e. hanged, period. Not unlike what Anglo countries call "statutory rape".

其和姦刁姦者男女同罪. In case of consented fornication and seduction, men and women get the same penalty.

姦生男女責付姦夫收養. If fornication results in a birth, the male fornicator must raise the child.

姦婦從夫嫁賣, 其夫願留者聽. If the female fornicator is married, her husband can sell her to someone else, or keep her if he so chooses.

若嫁賣與姦夫者姦夫本夫各杖八十婦人離異歸宗財物入官 If she is sold to the male fornicator, the fornicator *and* the cuck husband each get 80 strokes of the big stick. The woman is sent back to her father and her property is impounded by the government.

強姦者婦女不坐 Raped women have no punishment.

若媒合容止[人在家]通姦者各減犯人[和刁]罪一等. People who promote or provide lodgings for fornication get the same punishment as fornicators, with one degree less. So 70 strokes of the big stick instead of 80.

[如人犯姦已露而代]私和姦事者各減[和刁強]二等. People who, knowing fornication took place, do not denounce it to the authorities and instead helps the parties reach a private agreement, get the same punishment, with two degrees less. So 60 strokes of the big stick.

This part is important.

其非姦所捕獲及指姦者, 勿論. If someone claims there was fornication but didn't actual caught them in the act, there is no crime.

若姦婦有孕[姦婦雖有據而姦夫則無憑]罪, 坐本婦. If a female fornicator is pregnant, she alone is punished. After alone, there is proof of her deed, but not of the man's.

> Again, you needed proof, which wasn't easy to come by. After the main articles come some further detailed regulations.

條例

一、凡職官及軍民姦職官妻者, 姦夫、姦婦女並絞監候. If a public official or military man fornicates with the wife of a public official, both male and female fornicator hang.

若職官姦軍民妻者, 革職, 杖一白的決. If a public official fornicates with the wife of a military man, he is fired and gets 100 strokes of the big stick, [maximum penalty]. In this case the sentence had to be executed, he couldn't evade it with money (as normal penalties could).

姦婦枷號一個月，杖一百. Fornicating military wife must carry the cangue for a month, and 100 strokes of the big stick.

The cangue was a square made of wood with a hole for the head, or sometimes the hands, which people couldn't get off. It's basically a very funny way of making everyone know you're a criminal. In this case a huge slut.

其軍民相姦者，姦夫、姦婦各枷號一個月，杖一百. If two military people fornicate, they get the cangue for one month, and 100 strokes of the big stick.

其奴婢相姦，不分一主，各主，及軍民與官員，軍民之妾婢相姦者，姦夫姦婦各杖一百. If two servants fornicate, whether they belong to the same master, or have different masters, as well as when military men fornicate with the concubine of a military men or a public official, both fornicators get 100 strokes of the big stick.

- Note that simple fornication between free people was 80 strokes. -

凡有輪姦之案，審實，俱照光棍例，分別首從定擬.
For cases of gang rape, after investigating the truth, officials must follow the Thug Regulations, and sentence separately the leader of the gang and the followers.

> The Thug Act being apparently Qing Dynasty official jargon for a special law for hoodlums and petty gangsters that the dynasty set up pretty early on. A principle of that law was to punish gang leaders with immediate beheading, and followers with deferred hanging. I guess the idea was to get the followers to rat on each other with the hope of having their death sentence annulled before Hanging Season started in the fall. -

The following article was about 雞姦, literally "chicken fornication", which my dictionary tells me means "sex between men". That I think is matter of another post.

My classical Chinese isn't perfect and my legalese is even worse, so if there's any error please let me know. But I think my translations are decent. I hope you get the gist of the law. Sex happens within marriage; period. If you must fornicate, at least take care that nobody knows or cares.

38 - Historic China

The Water Margin

40 - Historic China

Male culture

2015-09-30

So I'm reading the *Water Margin* (Shui Hu Zhuan 水滸傳). Written in the 15th century, it's the most famous vernacular novel in Chinese history, together with the *Romance of the Three Kingdoms*.

Well, I'm not actually reading it (it's *long*). I'm watching the 2011 TV show. Which is long too, but very neat. The Water Margin is the story of 108 men. Good men, strong, noble, virile men who are wrongly abused by the governmenet, and thus rescind their loyalty to the state, and run to the hills to form bands of bandits to fight for their manly honor. The story is based on the Song Dynasty, particularly the reign of the infamous Huizong (1082-1135), who was so fucking awful he deserves a post for himself. The novel is fiction, often very, very wild fiction; but it is loosely based in actual events on the era. There's an earlier novel about evil bandits in the mountains doing evil things. The Water Margin tripled the characters, and made them into good, noble men. It also sold like crazy, becoming the second most famous novel in the world, while it's more truthful predecessor was forgotten for 900 years.

42 - Historic China

The Song Dynasty gets a lot of good publicity for being wealthy, commercial and urbane. Indeed the Chinese economy boomed like it never would until well into the 19th century. The Song state also solved the problem of military warlords running petty kingdoms in their domains; the exam system became the only path into officialdom, and the strengthened mandarinate run a tight administration without obstruction by the army, the eunuchs or the palace women. Obviously the Confucian establishment, to this day sees the Song Dynasty as the golden age of sagely government and efficient bureaucracy.

But that's, of course, bullshit. The Song state was plagued with bureaucrat factionalism, corruption and anarcho-tyranny. In fact the Water Margin is, if anything, a 960,000 word story of anarcho-tyranny, 850 years before Sam Francis had to coin the word for Western audiences. The Song bureaucrats who run the country were only concerned in grabbing taxes from the populace, and use them to bribe their superiors to strengthen their purses and factions; while wide swathes of the country were left to bandits to roam and rob all the caravans that passed close by. The law was enforced inasmuch as it the act may benefit a particular bureaucrat; else who the hell cares. And who is going to check? Everybody has their backs covered by powerful faction leaders at court. And so our 108 heroes were, oh so against their wishes, into lawless banditry.

There's of course lots to talk about the Water Margin, and how it reflects the values of lower-middle class Chinese during the last 1,000 years. I'll write about a couple of stories that reflect how they thought of women. Feminism of course is one of the biggest problems of modern Western culture, so it's useful to see how another powerful culture thought of women and how they should be treated.

Now, Chinese literature is pretty good; but it has never done well abroad because Chinese names just don't sound human in European languages. It's very hard to relate to Zhao Gao grabbing a deer to Huhai. Hamlet killing Polonius on the other hand sounds great. And Leonidas fighting Xerxes is pure awesomeness. So I'm going to change the names of the characters to Homeric ones chosen at random, and will put an annex showing the real names for those interested.

One of the most famous stories on the Water Margin is the story of Cassandra. Cassandra was a servant in a wealthy household. She was also extremely beautiful, famous around all the province. The master of her household, not surprisingly, took a like at the girl, and tried to take advantage of her. She, surprisingly, wouldn't have it, and went to the master's wife to rat on her master.

Which was a very stupid thing to do; as the wife couldn't really do much about it, and the master got real pissed at this uppity servant. So he decided to give her away on marriage to the ugliest guy of the province. He went all the way to find an ugly, hunchbacked, and dirt-poor street seller of steamed buns, and gave Cassandra to him for free (Traditionally Chinese girls were given in exchange of a hefty bride-price). The ugly street peddler, Ennomus, couldn't believe his luck, and took this beautiful and smart lady with him.

This arrangement though just couldn't work out. She was predictably miserable, hated her unfortunate fate, and wouldn't let Ennomus touch her. All the town was rife with gossip about the ugly poor peddler with the hot wife, and all the cool youngsters on town routinely harassed him, and went to his house to try to grab her from his house. "Such a fine piece of mutton, how did it get into the dog's mouth!". Soon there were rumors that Cassandra was banging one of the cool kids, and Ennomus decided to move to a different county to avoid the dishonor.

So moved they did, and soon good fortune visited Ennomus. His younger brother, Amphimachus, came back home after years of absence. While Ennomus was short, ugly and just plain disgusting, Amphimachus was 6'5" tall, handsome, strong, muscular, extremely virile and the best fighter in the whole province. He was also a prodigious drinker, and after drinking 30 jars of wine, he encountered a tiger in the forest, who he, pissed drunk though he was, killed with his bare knuckles. "Tiger-killer

Amphimachus" was soon the sensation of the province, and the local governor hired him as chief of police. He was also a very filial brother, extremely happy to meet his brother Ennomus, who had raised him as a child, they being orphans. So Ennomus know had the coolest guy on earth living with him. Now let's see who dares joke about him and his hot wife!

Indeed nobody dared joke about the wife of the Tiger-killer's brother. Poor Cassandra was also very happy. What a handsome brother-in-law! Seems fate hasn't abandoned me. Sheesh, why wasn't I given to him and not his hunchback brother. But hey, he is living here, right? If, you know, something were to just happen between us, what could Ennomus do about it? He certainly wouldn't dare fight his brother. And with a little bit of luck ew could even sign some transfer contract or something.

Alas Amphimachus is, as all the Water Margin heroes, a Good, Noble, Virile man. In the original, literally a hero-good-man. **英雄好漢**. And hero-goodmen just don't care about women; certainly not about filthy sluts. There is nothing more dishonorable than touching one's brother's woman. And so Amphimachus told Cassandra, after pushing her to the ground. "Either you stop being such a slut, or the next time I see you, my eyes may recognize you, but my fists will certainly not!".

Oh poor Cassandra. The hot brother-in-law wouldn't take her, so she was back to daily life with her poor,

46 - Historic China

disgustingly ugly husband. And I mean very ugly. The TV show makes a good impression of how miserable it must be to live with such a man, what a waste of beauty it was for her to be there. Fortunately she wasn't the only one to notice. Mecisteus, a scion of the wealthiest family on town, and a notorious womanizer, soon took notice of the beautiful Cassandra. And he just couldn't let it pass for such a beauty to be the wife of an ugly hunchbacked peddler. Oh no, that wouldn't do. As a lover of beauty, he had to do something.

Mecisteus used his wealth to bribe the governor into sending Amphimachus away on official mission. Then he got a local tavern owner to sneak Cassandra out of home with some womanly excuse, and he proceeded to bang Cassandra with abandon. Damn, she's hot. Mecisteus was happy. Ecstatic. He, with 5 wives, and a notch count in the 3 figures, just couldn't get enough of Cassandra. It might have been that she was also especially enthusiastic. Mecisteus, after all, was rich and handsome. And she really craved for a way out. Mecisteus promised to find a way to marry her. Cassandra wept with happiness. At last! Fate hasn't cursed me!

Problem is Cassandra was, well, married. And the hunchback wasn't going to divorce. Not even after the affair was found out, and he was made the laughing-stock of the whole county. Yes, being cuckolded was pretty much social death in ancient China. But... Cassandra was hot. Very hot. No way in hell he was going to find a finer woman if he let her go. Hell, no chance in hell he'd ever be able to buy himself a wife if she let her go. So no divorce for her.

That left only one option left. Kill the damn hunchback. Amphimachus is still away. Just poison the fucker and let's be done with this quick. And so Cassandra poisoned Ennomus. She then cremated the body, put on her mourning clothes and faked the whole ritual as good as she could. And then the feared Amphimachus came back. Came back to see his dear brother, who raised him as a kid, his only family, was dead. And there wasn't even a body to give offerings to. This evil bitch must be responsible. He soon found out the whole story, the rich Mecisteus, the affair at the tavern, the poison. Everything.

Tiger-killer Amphimachus, bursting with righteous rage, made all the neighbours gather at his brother's tomb, and in front of them grabbed his sword and killed the beautiful Cassandra. He then cut her head, and took it out with him. He headed to Mecisteus compound, which he burst into, and threw Cassandra's severed head into Mecisteus dining table. Fighting ensued, and Amphimachus also slayed Mecisteus, also severing his head. He then took the heads of the evil couple to his brothers tomb, and proudly told him, "brother, I have avenged you." He then went to the governor's office to give himself in.

48 - Historic China

This is one of the most famous pieces of the Water Margin, itself a classic in Chinese literature. It even served as the basis of a spin-off, the *Jin Ping Mei*, a classic novel in its own right, which tells the story of what would have happened if Cassandra and Mecisteus survived the endeavor, and actually married. My view of this story was that Amphimachus is an evil asshole. Yes, adultery is bad. But his brother had it coming. Cassandra and Mecisteus deserved each other. They were the perfect match. The pretty womanizer rich boy with the vain pretty girl. They loved each other, and looked great together. Ennomus only got Cassandra because her master was an evil bastard who gave her away as punishment. The marriage was so unbalanced that it was unhappy from the start, forcing him to move from his hometown. It was unnatural. It just couldn't work.

And yet when reality reasserted itself, the blockhead tiger-killer drunkard bro, who had seen too many Bruce Lee movies, rejected the hot girl's advances, and threw her away to the hunchback's arms. Of course she run away. And she wouldn't have killed Ennomus had he accepted the divorce. The greedy hunchback deserved the poison. Of course it sucks that your dear brother and only family gets killed. But as his brother he should have counseled him to divorce the slut and make a new life together. He could earn money to get her a new wife who suited him better. But no, the bro had to defend the "family honor". As a result 3 people died. Bad. Very bad.

But that's not the way that the Chinese see it. In the novel, the whole county is awed by Amphimachus show of prowess and his filial piety towards his brother. Instead of being executed, as the law demands for murder, he gets *cipei*, a tatoo in the face saying "prisoner", and a sentence of forced conscription in the frontier army for some years. The whole exile is a charade, as his former comrades are commissioned to send him off, and he has VIP treatment wherever he goes.

Cassandra on the other hand became the archetype of the evil slut, who can't control her lustful impulses and brings havoc to herself and her lover. Poor girl. Now this may be just me finding the actress on the show too pretty, and feeling undue compassion. But I still think her marriage was wrong to begin with, and she had a right to run away with whoever wanted to pay for her, without being beheaded by a drunk bro. But in China, the bro is in the right, and the unanimous opinion is that she deserved being brutally killed in public. Bros before hoes.

The obvious reason is that the lower-middle class Chinese who read and loved the Water Margin tales of brave bros fighting the government, were, well, lower-middle class bros with little access to women at all, while they lived surrounded by their menfolk. Large groups of young men hanging out often tend to produce very typical signaling dynamics: bros before hoes, binge drinking, martial arts, loud claims of unconditional loyalty. This works alright until there's real money or women involved; then everybody stops drinking and fighting, and starts betraying everyone else. Biology always wins.

Names:

Cassandra: 潘金蓮 Pan Jinlian

Ennomus: 武大郎 Wu Dalang

Amphimachus: 武松 Wu Song

Mecisteus: 西門慶 Ximen Qing

The Law

2016-04-14 // china, history, Song Dynasty, series, power

A while ago I wrote some posts on the classical Chinese novel, the 14th century *Water Margin* 水滸傳. The *Water Margin* is the story of 108 outlaws, in the original 英雄好漢, which literally translates as hero 英雄 *yīngxióng* and ... 好漢 *hǎohàn* is very hard to translate. 好 means good, that one's easy, but 漢 means, well, Han, the Han Dynasty, the Han race we know today. It also means man, today normally expressed as 漢子 *hànzi*. But not just man, that's 男 *nán*. A 漢 is a real man, a strong, manly man, respected by his peers. You call someone a 漢子 *hànzi* as a compliment, to mean he's a real man. Add 好 to that, and you have a good+real man. I'd translate it as dude, for lack of a better fit, and also because it fits with the whole LARPing atmosphere of the men in the *Water Margin*.

They're just a bunch of outlaws, some with good reason, fleeing from the injustice of tyrannical government, some who lost their families to evil but connected people. Others though are just punks and hooligans; small time robbers, mountain bandits, drunkards, smugglers, that kind of people. That they spend the time calling each other great heroes is quite hilarious. Still, China has a long tradition of vagrancy and men doing their own thing, i.e. learning martial arts and forming gangs of bandits. Not everyone could pass the mandarin exam, you know. And those mandarins in the government didn't have the resources to police the whole country, so there was always very easy to hide in the mountains and make a living of highway robbery. If you got very big, chances were the government would give up on arresting you, and would rather take it easy and give you an official position in the army or government. Once an outlaw became a Mandarin he was way easier to arrest or even assassinate as expedient. Never bet against the government.

There are tons of great stories in the *Water Margin*, and one of the most interesting is the story of Chái Jìn 柴進. Mr. Chai, or Lord Chai as he is usually called, is a very rich guy, who gets into the novel because he becomes the patron of many of the outlaws in the novel. He says he enjoys "meeting hero-dudes", whom he houses and feeds in his compound for months at a time, while having them fight each other. Kinda like patronizing wrestlers in your house and have them put a show for you every now and then. Mountain banditry is fun, but there's not always enough to rob, and the government is always trying to kill them, so they tend to look for wealthy patrons who can feed them during bad times, and protect them from the police, who won't dare disturb wealthy aristocrats. Wealthy aristocrats also find it useful to have a bunch of goons at their disposal.

Lord Chai in the novel appears as a very high class, cultured man. He owes his position as his being the direct descendant of Chái Róng 柴榮, the last emperor of the Later Zhou Dynasty. The history goes like this. Remember that the *Water Margin* is based in the 1100s. Centuries earlier China had the Tang Dynasty, glorious apogee of imperial China from 618 to 907. After the Tang empire collapsed, China fractured in a dozen or so little kingdoms, constantly fighting each other, in an era called the Five Dynasties and Ten Kingdoms period. At the end of that big civil war, one of the big warlords started to get the upper hand, and founded the Later Zhou Dynasty. It's second emperor was this Chái Róng, and he managed to conquer almost all of North China.

Chái Róng was a military genius, a real leader of man, and he appeared poised to conquer the whole of China and restore a unified empire. But then he died. 38 years old. Damn. He left a heir, a 6 year old boy, who of course had never left the palace, and was under the control of his mother and a bunch of ministers, eunuchs, sycophants and all that. The army wasn't happy with having a bunch of bookworms and women running the show. Especially because the first thing that the new government did was send the garrison at the capital out to the war front, with the obvious intent of having them killed, so they could purge the capital and put new, loyal men in their place.

The head of the palace garrison, Zhao Kuangyin 趙匡胤, was of course very close to the late emperor Chai Rong, which is why he was in charge of the palace troops. The new regent government sent him out to the front to fight the Khitans, the Mongols of the day. He of course marched on, but on crossing the first bridge out of the capital, his troops mutinied. It went something like this, I translate very liberally:

"My general, it's obvious that the new government wants you killed. Which is cool, but that means that all of us have to get killed too, and we'd rather not die, if you don't mind."

"What do you suggest then."

"We got you a yellow imperial robe, so put this on and let's go slaughter those eunuchs in the palace and put you as emperor."

"Wow wow wait a minute. What?"

"Look, you can do it, or your brother will. He's rather keen on the idea."

"Mmm ok."

And so General Zhao got his army, run back to the capital, staged a coup, and declared himself emperor of the Song Dynasty, which was to (mostly) reunify China, and last 319 years, 960 to 1279. Note that the events of the coup at Chen bridge are my personal interpretation. Officially he was drunk, his officers put the robe on him by force, he was reluctant but his officers didn't leave him much of a choice. His brother is said to have "persuaded him". I wonder how. He eventually murdered him and became the second emperor of the dynasty, by the way.

Anyway, General Zhao starts the Song Dynasty, which is the dynasty under which the events on the *Water Margin* unfold. Usually in China the founding emperor of a Dynasty leaves a set of ancestral rules, to be followed by all his descendants. One of the rules the first emperor of the Song Dynasty set was "Be nice to the Chái family." Zhao Kuangyin owed all he had to the patronage of Chai Rong, but he had just usurped the throne from his 6 year old son. He had good reason to do so; but he understandably felt guilty about it. So he left it as Ancestral Law, that the Chái family were to given privileges in all eternity. They were given an Iron Plate, which basically said that government officials had no right to enter their house premises, nor could they be put to death or torture under any circumstances.

And 5 generations or so later we get to Chái Jìn, who is the holder of the Iron Plate, and uses it to make hero-dude friends, who love the extraterritorial privilege of their house. Ostensibly, Lord Chai uses his privilege to make friends with good, virtuous men, who have been oppressed by evil government. So his house is a refuge for good men, and eventually becomes a base for the virtuous movement against corruption and tyranny. Which is the point of the whole book, our 108 herodudes rebelling to clean the government from evil and corrupt ministers, and restore power to our great Emperor, who of course knows nothing about it. Nothing at all.

Anyway, eventually the uncle of Lord Chai gets into a fight with some punk in his town, and eventually dies of his injuries. Lord Chai gathers up his herodudes and goes beat the guy who killed his uncle, and they beat him to death too. But apparently that punk was no ordinary punk. Else he wouldn't have dared touch the uncle of Lord Chai, of course. It happens that punk was the brother in law of the county governor. The county governor was of course livid at a relative of his beating beat to death. He mobilized the whole government forces, and went up to Lord Chai's house with an arrest warrant.

But wait, doesn't Lord Chai have the Iron Plate? Given by the imperial house itself? You can't touch the guy. It's against the law.

Well, as it happens the county governor was the cousin of Gáo Qiú 高俅, an imperial minister and very close friend of the emperor himself. Whatever the Iron Plate says, the county governor had a relative in high places. That means that he could do as he pleased. Yes, Lord Chai had the Iron Plate. But so what? News of his attacking an Iron-Plate holder will never get to the emperor, he'll take care of that. And in the event that the emperor does get to know, what is he going to do? Go against his best friend because of some 200 year old law? To defend some guy he doesn't even know about? No chance. Lord Chai was arrested and tortured alongside his whole family, and his large estate taken from him.

Of course the herodudes on knowing of this event rushed off to his rescue, conquered the whole county and killed all the evil officials they found, and then some. Lord Chai was rescued and joined the herodude fortress base at Liang Shan, where he realized how The Law works.

And how does the law work? The law is just a piece of paper, or in this case a piece of iron. It does nothing by itself. It's power depends on people enforcing it, people with weapons. But why do people enforce it? Because it's their job, you'll say. But that's not how it works, is it? Your job description is yet another piece of paper. Your real job, in any organization, is to keep your boss happy. To do that you're often supposed to do what's written in your job description. But it doesn't necessarily need to be so. Sometimes your boss wants something else, and if you wanna keep your job, you better do what he wants.

That people generally are asked to do their job descriptions and not something else, depends on the fact that your boss likely has another big boss on top of him, and other fellow bosses alongside him, who compete with him on getting favor from the big boss. If your boss asks for you something that you're not in theory supposed to do, some other middle-boss may tell big-boss about that, and then he's in trouble. Unless big-boss is in league with the whole thing too, in which case it's the squealing middle-boss is in trouble.

The law gets enforced because the people in power want in enforced. If they don't want it enforced, it doesn't. Border security is the law. It's not enforced. Firing employees for being opposed to gaymarriage isn't in the law. But it does get enforced. As Moldbug said of the Constitution, either a law reflects the will of the powerful, and it's thus superfluous, or it doesn't, and is then deceitful. It's not that simple in practice: putting things to writing is not superfluous. It creates a small milepost, a Schelling point, which people can point at in order to use in their status competition. But it only works so far as people in power find it useful, or there's a culture which upholds respect for agreements beyond their actual use.

China never developed any tradition of jurisprudence, because they understood this very principle of politics. I sometimes think that the Chinese were too smart and realistic for their own good. Delusion can be good. The rule of law is pretty great if it works. Europe conquered China, not the other way around. But again, delusions only last so long, and in the end reality always asserts itself. The rule of law is dying in a way that wouldn't surprise the author of the *Water Margin*. Meanwhile China keeps being China. As Aldous Huxley wrote in one of his travel diaries:

I have seen places that were, no doubt, as busy and as thickly populous as the Chinese city in Shanghai, but none that so overwhelmingly impressed me with its business and populousness. In no city, West or East, have I ever had such an impression of dense, rank richly clotted life. Old Shanghai is Bergson's elan vital in the raw, so to speak, and with the lid off. It is Life itself. Each individual Chinaman has more vitality, you feel, than each individual Indian or European, and the social organism composed of these individuals is therefore more intensely alive than the social organism in India or the West. Or perhaps it is the vitality of the social organism - a vitality accumulated and economised through centuries by ancient habit and tradition. So much life, so carefully canalised, so rapidly and strongly flowing - the spectacle of it inspires something like terror. All this was going on when we were cannibalistic savages. It will still be going on, a little modified, perhaps by Western science, but not much-long after we in Europe have simply died of fatigue.

60 - Historic China

Proverbs

62 - Historic China

Stuff White People do

2012-12-05

The Chinese in their ancestral wisdom, have proverbs for every single situation. In fact one of the hardest parts of learning the language is their reliance on idioms, which tend to be verbatim quotes of classical works. 3000 years of writing in the same language means there's a vast pool of wise insight and sharp wit to choose from, but the old language isn't intelligible as such, so you have to memorise the idioms by rote. Once you do though, you literally have a comeback for everything.

It's so much part of the culture, that the tradition doesn't only rely on classical texts. Chinese are prone to make up idioms in the vernacular just as often. There is one I particularly like, which describes people who do pointless stuff. Some time ago Xi Jinping, the recently declared big boss in China, had these words to say[5]:

有些吃饱了没事干的外国人，对中国指手划脚.

This was translated by the South China Morning Post as: "Some foreigners with full bellies and nothing better to do

---

[5] https://www.youtube.com/watch?v=rtw32rdaik0

engage in finger-pointing at us". The translation is quite literal, and pretty good as it is. The point on this sentence is "full bellies and nothing better to do". This is the standard way of describing people who do something pointless out of what it's assumed is too much leisure. As any beginner learner of Chinese knows, full bellies in China used to be a very uncommon sight, to the point that people used to greet each other by saying: "Have you eaten yet?".

There's a variant to the saying which I like better, 吃饱了撑的, which means eating to the point of feeling stuffed. The Chinese consider it the root cause of all nonsense. Americans today would say you're full of shit. Kinda gross if you picture it, but the association with fullness is there. As far as folk wisdom goes, Catholic countries also have this (quite accurate) stereotype about priests being always fat gluttons. They are also not known for making much sense either.

Personally when I think of food and priests, I don't picture a fat Italian in a black gown eating too much spaghetti. No, I picture something more modern, yet consubstantial (to use catholic jargon). I think of...

Moldbug called our ruling class the Cathedral. And if you think about it, the economics profession has the most in common with the old medieval priesthood. They are generally smart, well educated people who are trained for up to a decade in what amounts to pure nonsense. They memorise the nonsense, and then use advanced logic to write down complex arguments and debate it with their peers. But only with their peers, their non-peers are commanded to shut up and obey.

Another proof that economics and priests are the same thing is that they end up talking about the same things. See this post at Chalupas Central[6]. They are talking about the poor, and conclude that it's about Ego Deprivation. Well I don't know what Ego Deprivation is. My gut tells me it's as pointless as Homoiousia. Now fortunately many commentators are refuting the pointless drivel that gets economics researchers paid, but then some comments make you lose faith in the powers of reason.

> *Trailsplitter November 27, 2012 at 7:56 am*
>
> *It is because of posts like this that I love this blog. Thanks Alex!*

Oh well. I do get that Economics was founded by Adam Smith, who was pretty close to becoming a priest, and his real job was moral philosopher. So yes there's some overlap between morality and macroeconomics, and

---

[6] `https://marginalrevolution.com/marginalrevolution/2012/11/attention-scarcity-ego-depletion-and-poverty.html`

economists are entitled to be concerned about "the poor". But Adam Smith, who was the real deal, a priest candidate, and did moral philosophy, surely didn't conclude that poverty was about Ego Deprivation. In Chinese folk terms, it follows that he didn't have a full belly. Which is quite likely. As ghastly as British food is today, in the 18th century it must have been really terrible. No cheap ethnic food indeed.

The Chinese saying was of course born in China, a society famously always lying in the Malthusian edge. It wasn't easy to have a full belly in China, and those who did it were of a particular class. Mostly government bureaucrats, who were of course chosen in a famously competitive civil service exam. My feeling is that Chinese masses developed the impression that smart people tend to spout quite a lot of nonsense, and they having passed the examination, hence being smart, the only reasonable cause must be that they had too much food. Which is a quite reasonable conclusion. But what if it's not about food?

See probably one of the highest IQ blogs out there, Robin Hanson's Overcoming Bias. I use to like much of what's written there, but they also post a considerable amount of crap. See this post of a while ago.[7]

---

[7] https://www.overcomingbias.com/2012/11/invent-yourself-and-think-through-your-impact-graduation-ceremony-speech.html

One of the things I do when I find something hard to understand is trying to translate it into another language. Say, Chinese. I usually find it quite hard to do, if not outright impossible. This is one of the beefs I have against Chomsky and his theory that all languages are superficial representations of an underlying 'mentalese' which is hardwired into human brains and thus universal. Well it's not that impossible to word by word translate "Invent yourself and think through your impact". I can do it. But it wouldn't make any sense in the target language, because they just don't think that way. They don't have the concept. Concepts being culturally specific. Chinese don't go to college to "invent themselves". They go there to get a piece of paper that will enable them to make more money than otherwise. And when they graduate they certainly are not thinking about spending $700 in saving lives in Mozambique. 2 months salary! I imagine what a Tiger Mom would tell her daughter if she talked about the categorical imperative of sending $700 to some QUANGO in Mozambique.

Now it's funny that the Chinese would be attribute saying stupid things to eating too much, when China is the most food-conscious culture on earth. Chinese cuisine is famously good, and everything here is celebrated with food. Part of the disdain that Uyghurs have towards the Han is how the Han are always eating eating and don't know how to have fun. Fun meaning music and dancing.

But as much as the Chinese like to eat, in reality they aren't that fat (for now). Everyone knows that the fattest people on earth are the Anglos, and by a long shot. Which must mean they get full at higher rates than any other peoples on earth. And it shows. The first example was American, the second was Australian. Now let's see how full the Brits are. This also I got from a link at Chalupa's.[8]

Now I'm used to read macroeconomic non-sequitur crap, and other moralising status-whoring by economists. But this piece on animal rights blew me away. This is not your run-of-the-mill unfalsifiable crap. This is way beyond that. This is the left singularity showing its teeth.

First of all, whose idea was it to put a close-up pic of the old lady on top? It's gross. You don't take close-up pics of old women. It's like asking the age of a 40 year old. You just don't do it. Nothing against this woman in particular, but old women are ugly by definition. A detailed close-up of an unrelated old human is bad taste.

Now what is this woman about? She studies animal behaviour. Which is a pretty interesting thing to study. We all like to watch funny animal videos at YouTube, and she gets to do that for a living. All she has to do is a write a paper once in a while. She could have stopped there, but of course she didn't. She had too much food, nothing

---

[8] https://edge.org/conversation/what-do-animals-want?

better to do, so she decided to apply her findings to study Animal Welfare.

I blogged on Animal ethics before[9], and I do find it a quite interesting subject. It's a big bleeding point in the European philosophical tradition, and as such it's the source of much hilarity. And corruption. So which is this old woman about?

Probably both, though I don't know. This woman is trying to make a case for animal welfare, and she does that by trying to link it with human self-interest. Of course that's not a moral argument at all. It's pure marketing. Fooling people into supporting something is not an argument for supporting it, it's just marketing. It's Sandra Fluke. But of course she doesn't care about the logic behind her case. She just wants to convince others. Anglo philosophy has long morphed from a system of logic and proof into a mere branch of public relations. How to manipulate people's psychology into supporting a thesis. Not that they will beat the Jews on that.

The second part of her case is defining what Animal Welfare is, which is no easy task. She rambles a lot about anthropomorphism, the idea that animals deserve welfare inasmuch as they are similar to humans. But she correctly points out that animals consciousness doesn't really exist

---

[9] `https://spandrell.ch/2012/02/28/on-ethics/`

in any provable way, so linking human psychology to animal psychology is quite impossible. So what's her solution? She defines animal welfare as giving animals what they want. Easy! Well, yeah. But in focusing on What Animals Want, what she's doing is applying standard liberal ethics (as per Jim Kalb's peerless analysis[10]) to the animal world. So in the end what she's doing is pure anthropomorphism but without justifying it.

She contrasts this approach with the naturalistic one, which says that animals should live as they would in the natural habitats. To what the old woman says:

A lot of people think that good welfare is when animals are allowed to perform natural behavior, and you can judge welfare by how natural it is. That's always seemed to me a little problematical because animals in the wild are regularly chased by predators, and that would be natural. I don't think one could actually argue that that was necessary for good welfare.

Well being eaten by a predator is certainly not What Animals Want, I'll grant her that. She also points out the practical consequences of that in farms:

this horrible thing that happens with free-range chickens, that they feather-peck each other. It's very distressing. People think doing away with batting cages will improve

---

[10] https://turnabout.ath.cx:8000/node

welfare. But in fact, you've got a whole new set of welfare problems associated with taking birds out of cages.

I think there's a very useful and profound (HBD-wise) metaphor in that. Not that she realises that of course. In the end, if you treat animals like humans, and give them welfare, you will get the same results as human welfare. Logic isn't that hard. Unless you have eaten too much, of course.

You can imagine what the Chinese think about animal welfare[11].

---

[11] https://www.squidoo.com/dogsinchina

Socialism qua Entropy watch

2012-12-08

Let me continue with Chinese proverbs.

We have established that the Chinese love eating, and they celebrate everything with a big feast with family and friends. So it's not surprise that gatherings with food are the metaphor for a good time. A famous saying (also vernacular) says:

天下没有不散的筵席

Which translates as: there's no feast where people don't leave in the end. Meaning basically, all good things must come to an end. I think there's a better, more funny way of saying that in English, but I can't remember right now. Any ideas?

I thought of this proverb after reading this news on Singapore's leading newspaper, the Straits Times.

Two workers from China charged for criminal trespass after crane protest[12]

---

[12] https://www.straitstimes.com/breaking-news/singapore/story/two-workers-china-charged-criminal-trespass-after-

The fact that the poor foreign workers have been detained and will probably be deported sounds like business as usual for Singapore. The Rule of Law. Everybody likes Singapore, right? Well look at the comments on the Straits Times piece. It has pearls such as this one:

> *Looking at the blank and dejected faces of the two Chinese workers, our heart cries for them. In the eyes of the law, maybe they have done something wrong but then if we are in the same shoes as them, we will equally be frustrated and embittered after coming so far away to slog and toil hard for a meagre salary, they are being cheated of their income. When they think of their family back home in the deserted rural area who is waiting for their monetary support to survive, their emotion distress will start to overwhelm them leaving them with no choice except to protest in public.*

> *The worst to come is seeing them being charged for criminal offense. Has Singapore law becoming so inhumane, so merciless and unforgiving that we have lost our touch of human compassion and humanity? Is a warning letter sufficient enough to settle such trivial issue taking into consideration this*

is their first offense and they are not harming anybody as far as we know.

This smells of... socialism! In Singapore? But it can't be! Singapore is a well-run place, right? It has rational governance? It has abolished politics, right?

You can never abolish politics. It's like abolishing sexual desire. For better or worse it's here to stay. Now you may say that I'm being specious, and many comments are for arresting the guys and kicking them out. I didn't go through all of them but I'd say the both sides are pretty even.

One thing that those pinnacles of civilisation, Singapore and Dubai, have in common is a reliance on cheap labor from abroad. Which works OK while you have an effective system to take the workers back once they cease to be useful. But you have to be careful with that. See another piece of recent news from Singapore.[13]

Two pieces of labor unrest in little less than a week must be quite disconcerting for the usually uneventful Singapore. But most disconcerting of all must have been that this news haven't been ignored in the drivers' homeland.[14]

---

[13]https://www.youtube.com/watch?v=uU-40YU8gqI

The Singaporean authorities, companies and the public have a lot to learn from this case. But more than that, Chinese workers who seek to work abroad should learn more about the country they go to and know how to get legal aid when they face problems.

The Chinese government now pays special attention to protection of Chinese citizens abroad. The Foreign Ministry and the Ministry of Commerce have expressed concerns over the strike incident, and the Chinese embassy in Singapore has communicated with the Singaporean authorities and workers.

The recent Report of the 18th Party Congress said: "We will take solid steps to promote public diplomacy as well as people-to-people and cultural exchanges, and protect China's legitimate rights and interests overseas." This case has highlighted the need for the government to take all necessary steps to protect the rights and interests of Chinese citizens working overseas.

Singapore has been able to withstand Cathedralist pressure against its legal system because nobody in the West cares or has any incentive to mess with it. But if China starts flexing its muscle and meddling with what it regards as its sphere of influence, well, things are going to get interesting. Singapore survives, and this was explicitly

---

[14] https://usa.chinadaily.com.cn/epaper/2012-12/06/content_15992183.htm

declared by Lee Kuan Yew himself, by leeching Chinese talent to offset the flight of its own talent to the US and Australia. But Singapore might not be able to secure it's newly leeched talent's loyalty if Mother China doesn't let go.

The best designed governance doesn't mean much if you don't have the power to enforce it. What can't continue will stop.

On Attrition

2012-12-14

I wasn't really planning on making a series on Chinese proverbs. But it happens that every time I start writing a post I can think up of a proper Chinese expression to introduce it. Such is the vastness of the language.

何苦?

This is not a proverb actually, but it is an idiomatic expression inherited from the Classical Chinese. Word-by-word it means "what bitter". Which is pretty ungrammatical. But Asian languages in general have quite flexible grammars, and Chinese more so. The expression usually translates as "why bother?", "why make things so hard"? Bitter is the Chinese word for hardship, hence Coolies 苦力 "bitter force".

It is a very frequently used expression, because Chinese have this habit of making things harder than they need to be. For all the talk about HBD having its future in the practical-minded Asian countries, East Asia is very much about effort. At least since Confucius, the key to success in China has been relentless self-improvement. There's two kinds of humans, "small people" 小人 and

Gentlemen 君子. They key to being a Gentlemen is having a good education. Fast-forward 2500 years and you have the Banzai-charges of Japanese army troops against the mechanised Soviet batallions in Khalkhin Gol. They lost, and didn't learn from it. This year there was a report on some US advisors to the Japanese army saying that their performance sucks because of a lack of fatigue management. They won't give the soldiers a break.

The obsession of Asians with pointless effort has become a popular topic of discussion with the increasing numbers of Asians in the US, and the ensuing bitterness for all the other kids who have to compete with them. Everybody hates those Asian kids in cram school getting straight As in topics they don't give a shit about. Just when people were starting to notice it, Amy Chua had her book, and the infamous article on the WSJ. Really exquisite timing. All in all it was a very interesting book. It's not often that Asians explain their own culture in proper English. And doing so in a conflicted tone, that one of someone who has properly assimilated to a Western culture, and can explain it on Western terms.

Still for all her explanations, the consensus is that she's a heartless bitch who mistreated her children, and all Asians parents are freaks. I won't comment on that. Moralising is cheap. I think you should judge things by their results. So what was the result of Amy Chua terrorising her children for a decade? Did she produce smart, polite, humble and tasteful kids?

Nah, she produced a run-of-the-mill overbearing, loud and full-of-herself liberal bitch.

Go check out yourself.[15] Lotsa pics of the chick in short skirts. The writing is impossibly annoying but the pics are nice. And very telling.

Amy Chua spent 15 years of her life filling her family life with fights and shouts and sheer unpleasantness... to produce yet another narcissistic liberal. Confucius would be proud.

---

[15] https://tigersophia.blogspot.com/

The purpose of absurdity

2015-06-03

Ron Unz had an interesting comment[16] at Sailer's blog a while ago:

> *Actually, another suspicion I've often had is that much of that massively-promoted total nonsense like transexualism and Gay Marriage is meant to flush out and expose potential troublemakers potentially lurking within ranks of the elite before they can rise high enough to become a serious problem. In support of this hypothesis, the leading purge victims are usually found within the fields of popular culture, entertainment, celebrity, and the media, which constitute a crucial chokepoint in controlling our society. It's obviously much easier and safer to detect and purge a future Mel Gibson while he's just a rising young actor than after he's spent a dozen years as Hollywood's #1 star.*

---

[16] https://www.unz.com/isteve/im-not-making-this-up-2/#comment-955678

the reason the King walks down the street naked in his imaginary suit is to draw out and catch those people unwilling to say they see what isn't there.

In an actual historical example, the Emperor Caligula appointed his favorite horse to the highest official government position in the Roman State. How better to break the spirit of potentially disloyal Senators and military commanders, and determine which of them might have independent thoughts.

Well put. But personally what struck me is that he had to come up with this by his own. A very intelligent man in his 50s had to personally realize this. When it should be a perfectly obvious point.

The very point of writing down history is to bring to make it easy for people to find out the patterns in human interaction, especially in politics, so that we can understand why things happen. Because the fact is that the same things happen all the time.

As I often say, all things considered, the best historical tradition in the world is that of China. The imperial government has put lots of people and resources into writing history there for 3,000 thousand years. And one of the results of this emphasis is that they have left a lot of interesting stories about important patterns in political history, often in the form of neat 4-letter idioms.

By making them into tiny and neat idioms, you make them much more accessible to the public's memory. Which is why any decently educated Chinese knows what 指鹿為馬 *zhi lu wei ma* means.

Letter by letter it is "point deer make horse". It tells the story of Zhao Gao, one of the closest ministers of the First Emperor of Qin. The Qin Emperor died in 210 BC, and soon after the Chen Sheng rebellion (another good example of history as a mirror for government) started, which in a few years destroyed the first empire that the Qin house had spent centuries to achieve.

Qin was able to conquer all the other Chinese states and build a unified empire because it had invented royal absolutism. Back in the 300s BC, Shang Yang had reformed the Qin government, stripped the landed nobility of all its privileges, and set up a centralized bureaucracy to effectively transmit the will of the royal house. A rationalized system of punishment and rewards made the peasants into very effective farmers and soldiers, and soon the other traditional feudal states were swept away by the absolutist Qin armies.

The funny bit is what happens with the royal house. As I said this was perhaps the worlds first absolute monarch ruling over a centralized bureaucracy. Well a lot happened to the Qin house during the years, but let's focus on the First Emperor. When he died in 210 BC, the crown prince, Fusu, was up in the army in the northern frontier. The emperor had died while touring the provinces, and with him was a younger son, Huhai.

Well the emperor died out of the capital, so nobody knew. The only ones who knew were his prime minister, Li S[i], and his close minister Zhao Gao, who may or may not have been a eunuch. Well apparently Zhao Gao didn't like the crown prince Fusu very much. He had reason to think that Fusu hated him, and would execute him as soon as he became emperor himself. So Zhao Gao gets Li Si and says "hey, dude's dead, we're the only ones who know. Fusu doesn't like you either, so why don't we get this kid Huhai and name him successor?"

Li Si took some convincing, as did Huhai himself. But eventually they got on the plan, and sent a forged imperial edict ordering Fusu to kill himself. Which strangely he did, even after opposition by his entourage. With crown prince Fusu out of the way, the three got back to the capital, and set up Huhai as Second Emperor of Qin.

Soon later Zhao Gao found some excuse and executed Li Si and all his family, and took his prime ministership. He obviously knew too much. Then he proceeded to execute all those little Schelling Points that were the emperor's brothers and sisters, so there was no contest about who had the right title to the crown. Still after Huhai was secure in his thrown, he was starting to be a little uncooperative with Zhao Gao. The Chen Sheng rebellion had started, and the empire was having trouble suppressing it. The Emperor blamed Zhao Gao for the mess and he had a point. But Zhao Gao didn't like that. He started to think that maybe they should have a change of emperor, but he couldn't be sure he could pull it off.

So Zhao Gao brings a deer into the palace. Grabs it from the horns, calls the emperor to come out, and says "look your majesty, a brought you a fine horse". The Emperor, not amused, says "Surely you are mistaken, calling a deer a horse. Right?". Then the emperor looks around at all the ministers. Some didn't say a word, just sweating nervously. Some others loudly proclaimed what a fine horse this was. Great horse. Look at this tail! These fine legs. Great horse, naturally prime minister Zhao Gao has the best of tastes.

A small bunch did protest that this was a deer, not a horse. Those were soon after summarily executed. And the Second Emperor himself was murdered some time later.

This story made it into the Records of the Grand Historian, by Sima Qian, around 100 BC, through which it became part of common knowledge for Chinese intellectual life. From then on, everytime somebody tried to pull off a similar stunt, opposing ministers could say "you're trying to say a deer is a horse, huh!", which could get other lukewarm ministers to wake up and support you. Or get you killed with your whole family.

In the West of course we have Hans Christen Andersen's tale about the kid and the emperor's new clothes. The funny part is it's fiction. And the story is just about a child, who having a pure heart, dares to say the truth against the powerful. The moral is that we should be ashamed of ourselves and aspire to be as virtuous as this child. But of course in reality this child would have been arrested and executed, alongside his parents. Which is obviously why nobody tells the king about his new clothes. They're not stupid.

This says a lot about Western sensibilities.

Giving the handle

2015-06-06 // china, history, power

My last posts were very well received. I guess there's a market for the intersection between Chinese history and Ron Unz, so here's another one.

Steve Sailer writes[17]:

> *As you may have noticed, Ron has this wacky theory that a surprising percentage of our political leaders have, shall we say, compromising incidents in their past. He even speculates that perhaps having something to hide from the public might make a rising politico more attractive to those who make it their business to decide which of the ambitious to help climb the greasy pole of political power.*

---

[17] https://www.unz.com/isteve/paging-ron-unz/

And he just had a new post[18] on what he's named the Unz Suspicion.

Mr. Unz is very right to suspect that much. But again Unz had to use all his powers of insight to come up with his idea. Which given his upbringing is quite impressive. And yet this has been common wisdom in China for thousands of years. A 10 year old in Kaifeng could have told you as much in 1034.

There's plenty of examples of great leaders of bureaucratic factions, imperial prime ministers who purposefully surrounded themselves with crooks in order to be able to crack down on any defector with ease. It may sound counterintuitive, but the group is much stronger if everybody is a crook with something to hide.

None of this is surprising given that China has had a continent-wide centralized bureaucracy for longer than the rest of the world combined. And while the world has changed a lot since 221 BC, and China itself has seen a lot of variation, the dynamics of bureaucratic power are basically the same.

I'll illustrate this point again with a 4 letter idiom, and one of my favorite stories, also from the first empire, the Qin

---

[18] https://www.unz.com/isteve/chinas-big-data-plan-for-acting-on-the-unz-suspicion/

Dynasty.. The idiom 授人以柄 *shou ren yi bing*, which translates as "handing over your (sword's) handle.

The idiom itself doesn't come from this piece of history. It comes from the Three Kingdoms period, when some nobles were discussing strategy, and argued against one idea saying that it was equivalent to 倒持干戈，授人以柄, holding our swords in reverse and giving the handle to the enemy. Which is a nice metaphor for a suicidal idea.

The idiom later acquired a figurative sense, where you *voluntarily* hand your sword's handle to someone, in order to signal your loyalty and lack of ambition. It's a fairly profound point. Let me explain.

So it's the late Warring States period. Qin is by far the most powerful state, and has been so for decades. It's generally just a matter of time until it decides to get rid of all the other states and unify the empire. In 247 BC a new king, Ying Zheng, rises to the Qin crown, and decides that it's time to finish the job. They send gold around to soften up the ministers and delay their defense policies, and then send Qin armies to obliterate them.

By the 225 there's only Chu and Qi left. Chu is in the way to Qi, so the decision is made to invade Chu first. But Chu is huge. It's mountainous, and it's full of people. It's not gonna be easy, so the King of Qin calls his best generals, Li Xin and Wang Jian, and asks what do they think it will take to win the war.

The King asks Li Xin, who says he needs 200,000 men. Then he asks Wang Jian, who says 600,000 are necessary.

"Six hundred thousand men! That's a lot of people. It's almost the entire manpower of the state. Wang Jian, I get you're old, but don't be so cowardly. See here young Li Xin, brave and bold who can do more with less."

And so Li Xin set forward to Chu with 200,000 men, in two columns. Wang Jian was so pissed that he actually quit his job and retired to a remote house in the mountains. Damn punk, 200,000 men huh. Right. What the hell do you know.

And what do you know, the Chu army plays a long game of retreat, retreat, retreat, Li Xin gets cocky, pursues too long, and bam, massive ambush, the whole Qin army is killed, Li Xin barely escapes with his life, and the Chu army starts to advance West with their eyes set on revenge.

The Qin King was furious, obviously. He had no choice but to go personally visit Wang Jian at his retirement home, and beg him to come out. Hey guy, sorry I called you old and useless. You were right. So go there and fight. Please.

"Ok, but 600,000 men."

"Yeah, whatever, just go."

So Wang Jian leads the biggest army perhaps in the history of mankind, and goes to attack Chu. The King escorts him personally to the border. Wang Jian asks him for lots of money, good farmland, mansions, women and treasure. It's for my children, you see. I want to secure their future. The King laughed heartily. Of course, old Wang. Whatever you want. Just win this war.

While on campaign Wang Jian send a messenger to the court every single day, reminding the king that he wanted lots of good farmland, gold, women and treasure. For his children. His entourage was getting embarrassed already. Come on general, since when are you so corrupt? Even if you are, just try to be subtle, this is ridiculous, you're making us all feel bad.

"You don't get it", says General Wang. "The emperor is a suspicious man. He doesn't trust anyone. Right now I have under my command 600,000 men, the entire army of the country. Every once in a while he must be asking himself:"What if this Wang Jian guy rebels against me?". And even if he doesn't ask himself, there's always an annoying eunuch paid by a rival general trying to backstab me, saying that I am famous and honorable, and that the opposition might rally around me, that I'm too powerful and must be killed sooner rather than later. Only by openly displaying that I am a vile, corrupt character who only cares about money, can I make the king trust that I have no higher ambition."

And so Wang Jian kept sending messenger asking for stuff, and the King never suspected his loyalty. He *liked* his pettiness. Wang Jian went forward to invade Chu, destroy its armies, capture his king, and annexed the country into the soon to be Qin Empire. He went back home, and very unusual in a famous general, died a peaceful death.

Sometimes you really have to hand over your sword's handle.

To this day, "having a handle" means knowing the secrets, or having the means to control someone to your benefit. People without handles, i.e. good people, are regarded as undesirable associates, at least in politics.

And yes, having databases, or at least long lists with compromising information about government officials has been a staple of Chinese politics for centuries. It's quite obviously the best way to keep a faction together. MAD, also, is a very old trick.

So nihil sub sole novum. Or in other words, **天下無新事** .

Names

2016-06-07

This has been going around.[19] Guess I should say something. I really don't know how to comment on that pile of nonsense. I might as well let the sages do it for me.

子路曰：「衛君待子而為政，子將奚先？」

子曰：「必也正名乎！」

子路曰：「有是哉，子之迂也！奚其正？」

子曰：「野哉，由也！君子於其所不知，蓋闕如也。名不正，則言不順；言不順，則事不成；事不成，則禮樂不興；禮樂不興，則刑罰不中；刑罰不中，則民無所錯手足。故君子名之必可言也，言之必可行也。

Confucius and his disciples were gathered at the master's house. One of his disciples, Zilu, asks the master.

Zilu: The Duke of Wei has asked for your opinion in how to rule his realm. He'll call you for an audience any time. What will be the first thing you tell him?

---

[19]https://marginalrevolution.com/marginalrevolution/2016/06/what-is-neo-reaction.html

Confucius: Oh, that he must fix the names.

Zilu: What? That? Oh come on, master, what does that even mean. "Fix the names". I don't get it.

Confucius: Shut up, you stupid brat, and listen. It is like this. If the names aren't correct, what you speak becomes nonsense. If you speak nonsense, you can't get things done. If you don't get things done, you can't get the rituals to work. If the rituals don't work, the law isn't applied as it should. If the law isn't applied as it should, the people can't make a productive living. When a ruler names something, he must be able to make sense when talking about it. And when talking about it, he must be able to do what he means.

My translation. Philosophy of language was a hot thing in China in those days. The topic was "names", not "words", but of course it's the same thing. Words are just names we put to things. Names we put to things for a reason. That reason should be to make communication more smooth, to make society work better.

Alas it works the other way around too. If you mess with words, if you use them in ways which don't make communication more smooth. If you lie and manipulate and make up bullshit constantly; well society goes to hell. But making society go to hell through the purposefully wrong use of language is a common profession in our days. Certainly it's the bulk of the work done by most of the academic establishment.

Correct Naming

2016-08-25

Master Xun (荀子 Xunzi):

夫民易一以道，而不可與共故。故明君臨之以埶，道之以道，申之以命，章之以論，禁之以刑。故民之化道也如神，辨埶惡用矣哉！今聖王沒，天下亂，姦言起，君子無埶以臨之，無刑以禁之，故辨說也。實不喻，然後命，命不喻，然後期，期不喻，然後說，說不喻，然後辨。故期命辨說也者，用之大文也，而王業之始也。名聞而實喻，名之用也。累而成文，名之麗也。用麗俱得，謂之知名。名也者，所以期累實也。辭也者，兼異實之名以論一意也。辨說也者，不異實名以喻動靜之道也。期命也者，辨說之用也。辨說也者，心之象道也。心也者，道之工宰也。道也者，治之經理也。心合於道，說合於心，辭合於說。正名而期，質請而喻，辨異而不過，推類而不悖。聽則合文，辨則盡故。以正道而辨姦，猶引繩以持曲直。是故邪說不能亂，百家無所竄。有兼聽之明，而無矜奮之容；有兼覆之厚，而無伐德之色。說行則天下正，說不行則白道而冥窮。是聖人之辨說也。詩曰：「顒顒卬卬，如珪如璋，令聞令望，豈弟君子，四方為綱。」此之謂也。

Which translates as:

The people can easily be unified by means of the Way, **but one should not try to share one's reasons with them.**

Hence, the enlightened lord controls them with his power, guides them with the Way, moves them with his orders, arrays them with his judgments, and restrains them with his punishments. **Thus, his people's transformation by the Way is spirit-like [i.e. religious].** What need has he for demonstrations and persuasions? Nowadays the sage kings have all passed away, the whole world is in chaos, and depraved teachings are arising. The gentleman has no power to control people, no punishments to restrain them, and so he engages in demonstrations and persuasions.

When objects are not understood, then one engages in naming. When the naming is not understood, then one tries to procure agreement. When the agreement is not understood, then one engages in persuasion. When the persuasion is not understood, then one engages in demonstration. Thus, procuring agreement, naming, demonstration, and persuasion are some of the greatest forms of useful activity, and are the beginning of kingly works.

When a name is heard and the corresponding object is understood, this is usefulness in names. When they are accumulated and form a pattern, this is beauty in names. When one obtains both their usefulness and beauty, this is called understanding names. Names are the means by which one arranges and accumulates objects. Sentences combine the names of different objects so as to discuss a single idea.

Persuasion and demonstration use fixed names of objects so as to make clear the proper ways for acting and remaining still. Procuring agreement and naming are the functions of demonstration and persuasion. Demonstration and persuasion are the heart's way of representing the Way. The heart is the craftsman and overseer of the Way. The Way is the warp and pattern of good order. When the heart fits with the Way, when one's persuasions fit with one's heart, when one's words fit one's persuasions, then one will name things correctly and procure agreement, will base oneself on the true disposition of things and make them understood, will discriminate among things without going to excess, and will extend by analogy the categories of things without violating them. When listening to cases, one will accord with good form. When engaging in demonstration, one will cover thoroughly all the reasons. One will use the true Way to discriminate what is vile just like drawing out the carpenter's line in order to grasp what is curved and what is straight. Thus, deviant sayings will not be able to cause disorder, and the hundred schools will have nowhere to hide.

One kind of person is brilliant enough to listen to all cases, but has no combative or arrogant countenance. He has generosity enough to extend to all sides, but does not make a display of his virtue in his appearance. If his persuasions are successful, then all under Heaven is set right. If his persuasions are not successful, then he makes clear his way but lives in obscurity—such are the persuasions and demonstrations of the sage. The Odes says:

Full of refinement and nobility,

Like a jade tablet or scepter is he,

So lovely to hear and lovely to see.

The contented and tranquil gentleman

Serves as a model universally.

This expresses my meaning.

Translation from Eric Hutton's Xunzi[20]. Pretty good translation, I must say.

And yes, Classical Chinese writing really is that short.

---

[20] https://www.amazon.com/Xunzi-Complete-Text/dp/0691161046/

The Song

Historic China

The Song Golden Age

2016-04-21 // china, history, Song Dynasty, series

People are asking for more Chinese history. I agree. Chinese history is great. It's long, it's well documented, and it's documented in explicitly moralistic terms. Chinese thought has been always focused in how to achieve good governance, and histories are written as to contain parables of what good government is, and what bad government leads to. The most valued history book in China, the *Zizhi Tongjian* 資治通鑒, written by Sima Guang in 1084, again explicitly states that it is to be an aid for emperors and mandarins to achieve good governance. Good government leads to nice things. Bad government leads to death and misery. That's all Chinese intellectuals have ever cared about. I think it's a good priority to have.

Sima Guang was a brilliant scholar, and it's a huge pity that he finished his book just before the best story in Chinese history happened. The Jingkang Incident of 1127. Oh man, that's such a great, great story. There should be more books about it. It's perhaps the most compelling story in the history of mankind. It's just so unbelievably simple, yet dramatic. It's so good it seems fiction. But no fiction is this good. Anyway, let me tell you this story. It'll probably take several parts.

So again, the time is the Song Dynasty, 960-1279. If you've been reading my posts on the *Water Margin*, you have some minimum background. The Song Dynasty was under many accounts the most wealthy and successful of all Chinese dynasties. Not to date; the best dynasty, period. Better than anything than came later. Richer, more urbanized, and arguably with better technology. The Song Dynasty had machinery that the Qing Dynasty didn't have in the 19th century. The Song economy had huge foreign trade links, and the Song government in 1000 again had higher revenues than the Chinese government in 1900.

Some argue that that was the result of better governance. As seen in the previous post, the Song had solved an eternal problem of Chinese governance: how to deal with the military and the aristocracy. The solution they took was to screw them both, and put the government completely in hands of the bureaucracy. They set up their model civil examination system, reduced the number of eunuchs to a minimum, took care the armies in the provinces didn't get too big, kept most of the imperial family in the capital so they didn't develop territorial power. I wonder if urban life was also meant to keep them busy having fun while depressing their fertility. Not a bad research idea.

Anyway, of course the obvious result of all that is that the army sucked balls. The Song army sucked really badly.

This is the first big Chinese dynasty, the Han dynasty, 202 BC - 220 AD. See it owns most of China proper, it also includes north Vietnam, north Korea, and the Tarim Basin, i.e. the Silk Road oases where today the Uyghurs live. It didn't start like that; the imperial territory was extended mostly by one guy, the emperor Wu (156-87), who was a truly amazing individual. I should write his story some day, but you could also watch 漢武大帝 which is an awesome show.

Anyway the Han Dynasty fell mostly when the Roman Principate fell. Like Rome too it kinda recovered once, but then they started fighting each other and the northern barbarians took over one half of it. Oh, parallels. And people say there are no patterns in history.

Anyway, Rome never recovered its glory, but China did unite again. It took a while, until the Sui Dynasty, but the whole thing didn't start working properly again until the Tang Dynasty (618-907).

The Tang owned all the Han did, and then some. The Tang owned the whole Mongolian steppe, Central Asia well up to the borders of Persia, not only north but a big chunk of South Korea. Now all that is, well, theoretical. The core Chinese land remained the same, everywhere else was populated by foreign peoples. But the Tang had beaten them militarily, every single one, and forced them to swear allegiance. It didn't take much for that allegiance to disappear; in about a century the Tang lost of all of

Central Asia, the Tarim Basin, Mongolia and Korea. But the Tang had managed once to crush everyone, fair and square. The Chinese still love to read about the great Tang Taizong and how he led the best Chinese armies ever to beat everyone up to Persia.

The Song were beyond small. They were by far the smallest dynasty in Chinese history. They lost Vietnam, which is still around by the way. They let a bunch of quasi-Tibetan herders, the Tanguts, grab the Northwest, the path to the Silk Road, land that had been Chinese for a thousand years. And they even lost the northern edge of the Chinese heartland, the land around Beijing today.

Beijing is at the edge of a huge plain. That's why the capital is there, to watch the mountain passes which divide China proper from the steppes at the north. You must control those passes, else the nomads come raiding whenever they want. Well, to be fair, the Song hadnt lost it, nor it lost Vietnam or all the others. All those lands were taken during the civil war after the Tang collapsed. The Song just failed to recapture them. The area of Beijing was taken by the Khitan, a dynasty of Mongolic herders, which as you can see in the previous map, was big, very big, and very very strong. The Song tried dozens of time but they couldn't dislodge them, nor could they beat the Tanguts, who were at most a bunch of ten thousand of herders. The Song was by far the smallest and weakest of all Chinese dynasties.

They didn't care though: they were swimming in money. Losing access to the Silk Road forced them to trade by sea: and surprise, maritime trade is much more profitable! The Song Dynasty had higher revenues in 1000 than the Qing dynasty had in 1900. Their technology boomed: by some accounts the Song had better machinery than the Qing 800 years later. Urbanization rates were also the highest China ever saw until the 20th century.

The Song were weak, but they were rich: they decided it was cheaper to pay off the barbarians than to keep an army to fight them. And it was true. What were the barbarians going to do with all that silver anyway? They naturally spent it in buying stuff from China. So the silver went away as tribute, and came back as trade. Better than to keep an army of uppity generals and risk that they stage a rebellion or blackmail the court every now and then. While a section of the bureaucracy was against such a dishonorable treaty, the smartest Mandarins knew that in order to keep running the government they'd better pay off the barbarians and keep the military from having any influence at court.

It was a massive diplomatic coup. It worked brilliantly. The Khitan were actually fairly civilized people. They were literate in Chinese, developed their own script based on it, run a fairly sophisticated state apparatus. The problem between nomadic herders and settled farmers is that nomadic life is hard. It's hard to live off animal products only. Nomads also want grain, cloth, paper, tea, you know, nice stuff. The only way of getting it is to trade or to take it by force. But the Khitan managed to invade a small bunch of Chinese land. It was enough for them; they got their small territory of Chinese land, full of Chinese farmers to make grain for them, Chinese scribes to run their government for them. The Khitan kept their capital north of the mountains, enjoyed their hunting and herding, and as long as the Song kept sending silver and silk, they respected a peace that lasted a 100 years.

The weakness of the Song solved the Mongol problem, allegedly for the price of the tax income of a single province. The army didn't like it, but the army could go to hell. At the Song it was the mandarins who run things. And they were doing a mighty fine job. The population doubled to more than 100 million people. Printing was invented and developed into a national industry, as well as gunpowder. Art and literature also developed beyond anything previous. It was a Golden Age. Some people say the Song were on the breach of undergoing a capitalist revolution.

And so we come to the reign of Huizong, the year 1100.

Huizong was a very refined man. He was a very skilled artist, and his paintings and calligraphy have survived to our time. His handwriting is regarded as one of the best in Chinese history, and I'm particularly fond of it. It must be fun to be able to write like that. I'd be writing stuff all day.

Being an artist and all that, the emperor wasn't very much into government stuff. He was more into the joys of life. He liked painting, writing poetry, drinking with friends, playing football (they played Cuju, which sounds incredibly hard but apparently was very popular back then). He was into women too. He famously didn't like the uptight hookers that got sent to his palace, so he had a tunnel built to go from the palace to the fanciest brothel in the capital so he could have fun like just any other aristocrat.

He was also into gardening. He had the fanciest stones in the realm be sent to him to decorate his garden. South China is full of this weird porous stones, and our emperor had a fancy for them. He had them brought from everywhere, and sent to the palace, rewarding who brought them with lots of gold. The thing is some of these stones were huge. China had canals all around its territory, so they could be relatively cheaply transported by water. But canals have bridges over them, and some of this stones just didn't fit below the bridges. So what did they do? These are Imperial Stones we're talking about. Rapacious bureaucrats who wanted to look good with the emperor had bridges demolished just so they could push the stones through to deliver to the emperor. The historical record is full of commoners wailing at the injustice. This is of course the time of the *Water Margin* and its peasant rebellions led by herodudes.

Huizong was also fond of weird animals. He had a part of his garden set up as a zoo, full with tigers, elephants and giraffes he had sent from Africa. In summary you'll have noticed that the emperor of the Great Song after 1100 AD is a fairly extravagant fellow. But hey, the Song is rich, they could afford a fanciful emperor. What they could not afford though is a stupid emperor. Because just as Huizong was having fun watching pandas battle with giraffes for bamboo at his home zoo, probably accompanied by some hooker, at this very moment his Khitan neighbors were in trouble. Very serious trouble.

The distribution of power

2016-04-19

Another Chinese story.

Royal absolutism was invented by Shang Yang in the Chinese state of Qin, 360 BC. Of course absolute rulers had existed before, in the Middle East obviously you had plenty of god-kings; but Shang Yang's governance was recognizably modern. It was planned on secular terms, it had a central bureaucracy, and it explicitly took power from the nobility in order to strengthen the authority of the central government. The way it was framed is that the King deserves to have all the power, that's why he's the king; and that the king having all the power will result in more Order and better government, as the people will have no power to resist and create Chaos. Later Chinese political thought changed a lot: Confucianism was explicitly against Shang Yang's ideas (what came to be known as Legalism). In fact one could think of Confucianism as the revolt of the upper middle class against the centralizing legalists. A sort of English or French revolution dynamic. Happens they lost; Confucianism only somewhat won in a very, very diluted way 300 later under emperor Wu of Han.

But the idea that the power of the Ruler should be absolute absolutely carried the day in Chinese political thought. That contrasts a lot with the Western tradition which since the Greeks is obsessed with Tyranny and Despotism and basically makes it hell to run a cohesive government. Power has to be shared or else Tyranny! Much of that was the spillover from the propaganda war on the Persian wars, where Greece was the Beacon of Liberty against the Persian Tyrant. Henceforth to be Greek meant to be against tyranny, because Persians. Then the Romans take over and the Romans were even more paranoid about central authority. They also had this trauma about the foreign Tarquins. The Romans really went the whole way by having two consuls which changed every year! That's crazy when you think about it. How can you get anything done? The only way the Roman state was able to remain cohesive is that the plebs were constantly agitating and salivating for the chance of slaughtering all the patricians, so the Senate must have been pretty cohesive.

An idea of the Western tradition of Liberty is that it was passed down from the old Indo-Europeans, who were a martial people. All men were soldiers, and men of arms tend to be very zealous of their honor and autonomy, if only in exchange of surrendering every time there's a war. I don't know how much that follows, though. The Chinese had their own martial tradition too; the Zhou order was a feudal order which started after the Zhou king distributed the empire's lands to his army buddies. Maybe it has something to do with pastoralism; but look at the Mongols. Then again the Mongols had been surrounded by China for centuries so maybe they got absolutism from there. It certainly didn't come naturally.

Anyway, China invented central bureaucratic government in 330 BC, but it only refined it in a strikingly modern way during the Song Dynasty, 960-1279. As I wrote in a recent post, the Song Dynasty was founded by the general of the palace troops, who staged a coup against his lord, presumably forced by his own troops. The first thing he did after assuming the throne was to gather one advisor of him and talk of the future. He asked him: "Since the great Tang Dynasty fell, we've been through 8 emperors already. Wars all over the place, the people suffering misery and death. Thing's messed up, how did all this happen?"

Minister said: "Oh man I so love that you asked that question. You're awesome my lord. The answer is quite simple: the problem is that the ruler has no power, but his subordinates have too much. The provinces are too strong. Take away their power, their funding, their best troops, and the very next day the realm will be in Order."

So the great founder of the Song Dynasty gathers his generals, who remember had semi-forced him to stage a coup and become emperor. He stages a sumptuous banquet and tells them:

"Gentlemen, if it weren't for you I wouldn't be here as emperor. Thing is, I kinda miss being just a general. Since I become emperor I haven't slept a good night's sleep."

His general buddies are startled, and ask: "Oh your majesty, how can you say that?".

The emperor responds: "Oh come on. It's obvious. Who doesn't want to take my place?"

The generals stand up, befuddled: "But, the Mandate of Heaven is yours, the realm is in peace, who could possibly even think of betraying you?"

The Emperor put a stern face and said: "Who doesn't want to enjoy glory and riches? Come on. Even if you didn't want to; if someday *your* troops come up, put a yellow robe on you by force, could you even refuse?"

That's of course exactly what happened to him. The generals were now speechless. Couldn't come up with anything to counter that. That's just obviously true. They got the message, started crying, kneeled down, and with their heads down shouted, sobbing:

"We are stupid for not thinking of that. You are right, please tell us how to solve this problem. Please let us live."

You might have asked yourself why they were crying. Thing is, the traditional way of solving this obvious problem had been to execute the new emperor's buddies one by one. The Han Dynasty famously did that with every single one of the generals who had conquered the empire for Liu Bang. The Song founder telling them this was not just logical argument. In normal circumstances this was the prelude for the emperor's pretorian guard rushing in and beheading them all on the spot.

The Song emperor wasn't that kind of guy, though. He told them:

"Life is short and hard as it is. Why not just grab some money, some land, fancy real estate to leave your children and grandchildren; get some fancy dancing girls to enjoy your old age. Spend the rest of your days drinking and laughing, without fights and grudges, isn't that the best?"

You damn bet it is. The generals took the offer and spend their rest of their lives enjoying the pleasures of life. The Song emperor then established the most rational and orderly central government in China. The civil service exam was set as the only path to officialdom, it's standards were raised, corruption was crushed. Exams were long, and hard. The answer sheets were anonymized; an army of scribes copied every exam by hand, so that the examiner couldn't recognize the handwriting. The imperial relatives received no privileges, the emperor intermarried with mandarin families. The army was crushed and rearranged so that no single general could mass any amount of troops nor spend enough time to develop any feelings of loyalty with them. Chinese history had been plagued with military rebellions. The Song Dynasty solved that problem for good.

As a result, the Song army kind of sucked. But that's a story for another day.

The Song Dynasty's Decline

2016-04-23

So we left the story at Song Huizong. Huizong was as I wrote a consummate artist and a famous *bon vivant*. He knew how to enjoy himself. That means he generally wasn't interested in politics. Politics is generally very boring, pushing paper around, taking decisions about stuff you know nothing about. However Huizong was very willing to do politics if the topic at hand was interesting enough; interesting enough for such a consummate artist, that is.

There is one topic he did like to discuss, which was *war*. Artists tend to like war. The glory of fighting, thousands of men armed to the teeth and killing each other in mass pitched battles. There's something aesthetically very striking about that and artists across the world tend to be very attracted to it. Huizong was no exception, he was very much into war.

The thing is the Song dynasty had been founded explicitly as a peaceful state. The Song founder had decided the army was more trouble than it was worth, so he instituted a meritocratic bureaucracy and let it run the state more or less unimpeded for 100 years. That results in unprecedented prosperity, the reign of the 4th emperor Renzong being regarded as the historical peak of Chinese government. That produced its own set of problems, though. While you may not be interested in war, war is interested in you. While the Khitans in the Northeast were quite honorable, the Tanguts caught notice that the Song had no army to speak of, so they started to harass the border in order to extract more money. The Song had to keep 1 million soldiers in the frontier, which weren't easy to pay. And the tax revenue wasn't getting any better. The commercial economy grew with the typical effects: rich getting richer, using their wealth to buy tax exemptions, the poor getting poorer, rising in rebellion every few years.

Things started to change when Huizong's father, Shenzong ascended to the throne in 1068. The guy was 19 years old. If 3000 years of Chinese monarchy have produced any lesson, the lesson is that young monarchs are trouble. They always are. Young people are by definition inexperienced, so they tend to do stupid stuff. And generally, young men like to fight. They are eager to fight. It's in their blood. Sometimes that turns out well, as Han Wudi who basically tripled the territory of China in 30 years and crushed every single army around it. But usually young emperors pick fights without thinking, and the outcome is catastrophic.

News of the Khitan troubles got to China's capital. Our artist emperor was of course ecstatic. At last! We should take advantage of that. All the sycophantic ministers proposed making an alliance with the Jurchens. Let them take all the barbarian land they wanted, in exchange of the Song taking back the northern edge of the Chinese plain and the mountain passes. The Jurchens agreed, but stipulated that the Song had to take the land they wanted by themselves. The Jurchens weren't going to do the job for them. Thus a formal alliance was achieved.

The whole thing stunk. For better or worse, Song China and the Khitan Liao Dynasty had been in peace for 100 years. The Khitans could've kicked Chinese ass any time they wanted, but they respected the treaty. Now that the Khitans were in trouble, the Chinese didn't wait a minute in betraying the treaty and stabbing them in the back. That wasn't a very nice thing to do. It wasn't very smart either.

Nobody told Huizong that, though, who was still having fun playing soccer and visiting hookers through his secret tunnel. In 1121 He ordered his closest eunuch, Tong Guan, who is famous as the only bearded eunuch in Chinese history, to command 150,000 troops and go straight to the southern capital of the Khitans, what is today Beijing. The Khitans in their steppe homeland were running from the Jurchens as fast as they could; surely they wouldn't hold in the south very long either.

But the Chinese were still just no match for the Khitans. The Khitan commander in the south, Yelu Dashi, who was also perhaps the most incredible heroes in this story, held the walls, struck back at the Song forces, and destroyed the whole army. 150,000 men, gone. The whole Song army vanished in what was supposed to be a cakewalk. The eunuch commander panicked. He couldn't just go back and say he didn't take the land! They execute you for that stuff. So he sent an envoy to the Jurchens, saying: "Hey, we're having some trouble here conquering the city. Why don't you come down yourselves and take it, in exchange you can have all the booty: the gold, the women, the children, take them all. We'll pay for all supplies you need. After you're done you leave and we'll take the land as agreed, right?".

Well, why not. The Jurchens found it to be a good deal, so they came back through the mountain passes, and conquered Beijing in a week. Grabbed the gold and valuables, took the local women as concubines, took the children as slaves, sent them back to the Jin capital, close to today's Harbin. Just in case you don't know, Harbin isn't a very comfortable place.

It was probably colder back then, and at any rate it was a wooden village. No gas heating. All the virgins of Beijing were going to be enslaved there thanks to the ineptitude of the Song armies. Ineptitude that didn't go unnoticed by the Jurchen armies on the ground. Remember they were supposed to hand the land over to the Song authorities. The Jurchens started discussing among themselves. "This guys suck, they couldn't take a single city that took us a week". But the Jurchen emperor, Aguda, was a man of honor. "We had an agreement, we'll stand by it. I'm not the kind of man that takes advantage of the weakness of others".

But then he died.

The Song Dynasty's Fall

2016-04-24

So let's continue the rise and fall of the Song Dynasty. Let me digress a bit and let me talk about the capital of the Song.

The Song Dynasty's capital was in Kaifeng. Kaifeng is probably the most retardedly located capital of all 3,000 years of Chinese history. Up until the Song, the capital of China had been alternating between Xi'an and Luoyang. Xi'an is in the Wei river valley, which is fairly narrow and easily defended if you control the mountain passes that surround the valley. Luoyang is just east of the mountains from Xi'an, in the North China plain proper, surrounded by mountains and a large river. Southern Dynasties had their capital at Nanjing, which is just south of the Yangtze river which is huge and completely impassable without a navy. And of course Beijing has been the capital for long due to its strategic location at the northern edge of the central plains.

But Kaifeng? It's in the middle of the damn plain! It has no natural defenses whatsoever. The only reason the Song capital is there is because the warlord who destroyed the Tang Dynasty 100 years later had his base there. Kaifeng is close to Jiangnan, the Nanjing-Shanghai area which is by far the wealthiest of the country, and the Grand Canal goes through there, so Kaifeng is well located to extract tax revenues from the rich areas. As such it had naturally grown to be a huge and immensely wealthy city, with over a million people. But military speaking it's a complete failure.

The emperor Huizong hadn't realized that, though. He was busy with his paintings, his zoo, his big fancy stones. His habit of bringing fine stones from the countryside had wrecked such havoc that just when the Jurchens were conquering the Khitan empire to the north, the Song had the huge Fang La rebellion which conquered the richest provinces south of the Yangtze. In fact the Song got to the invasion of the north 2 years later because they had to deal with so many peasant rebellions, all due to the fancy habits of our artist emperor.

Starting the war against the Khitans didn't help that. The state had to raise taxes and confiscate supplies in situ to feed the armies going north. That also started several rebellions in the northern countryside, which again also required military force to suppress. When all that was over, the Song army finally attacked the Khitan, and puff, 150,000 soldiers disappear in a single night. When the Jurchens came down to help out, the Song had virtually no army to speak of.

And so negotiations begin. The Jurchens declared that given that the Song had not fulfilled their side of the bargain, that they would't be giving away the whole territory they had agreed to. They gave to the Song about half of that. But well, what can you do. It's not like China was in a position to argue. A treaty was signed according to which the border was to be sealed, and any fugitive that crossed it was to be returned immediately.

Remember that the Jurchens were at most 2,500 cavalry men. That they had been able to conquer the Khitan was because they had taken over most of the Khitan armies, especially those made by minority groups. When invading the Chinese parts, most Chinese soldiers and officers employed by the Khitan surrendered to the Jurchen. One Chinese general who had surrendered to the Jurchen, on seeing the Song army occupying his neighboring county, decided to rebel against the Jurchen and declare his allegiance to the motherland, Song China. The Song commander was stupid enough to accept it.

The Jurchens were livid. They immediately sent an army to reoccupy the county, and the Chinese general fled to the Song controlled land. The Jurchens then demanded that the Chinese hand over the guy. The Song commander then, taking pity on his countryman, beheaded him with a clean blow, and sent the head over to the Jurchens. The whole thing was a PR disaster. The Chinese were dismayed at how weak and dishonorable the

Song army had been, giving away one of his countrymen after accepting his allegiance. The Jurchen swore that the Chinese would pay their breach of the treaty. You don't mess with Jurchens.

In 1123, the founder emperor of the Jurchens, now the Jin Dynasty 金朝, or Gold Dynasty, Wanyan Aguda died. The guy had had his glory, defeating his enemies the Khitans and taking over their empire; so he didn't press on the Chinese too much. But his successors wanted glory of their own. The Khitan empire was nice, but it was still a steppe empire. Not that much stuff in there besides sheep and horses. China, though, was rich and warm. And the Chinese were a bunch of lying bastards who deserved a lesson. The Song dynasty had been paying annual tribute to the Khitans in exchange for peace; the alliance treaty with the Jurchens stipulated that the Jurchens would inherit that tribute. When the Song failed to pay up in time, the Jurchens had had it. They decided to invade China.

It's 1125, and the Jurchens have effectively taken over the Khitan territory. In October 1125 the Jurchens rush south, and by February 1126 they are at the doors of Kaifeng. On their way they destroy everything they find, devastating north China. They reach the walls of Kaifeng and demand that the emperor, this Huizong they've heard about, respond for his treachery and breach of contract.

Now imagine our artist emperor must have felt. The guy had spent a life of carefree enjoyment of the most refined pleasures the earth had ever known. The best food, the finest silk, the best women, a personal zoo. Suddenly an army of savages from the forests of Siberia, two thousand miles to the north, is at the gates of the city asking for his head. Huizong panicked, wrote an edict blaming himself for all this problems... and abdicated on his first son. Then he made his luggage and fled to the south, where his ministers had promised he would be safe and could continue painting and playing soccer.

The son of Huizong, the new emperor, Qinzong (pronounced Cheen-tsong) apparently hadn't realized the gravity of the situation. 80,000 smelly barbarians at our gates? Nothing to worry about. Let's assault their camp during the night. And so the Song launched a massive assault to the Jurchen camp outside the gates. With the predictable result that the whole army was destroyed by the Jurchens. Who were now pissed. Very pissed. They demanded 5 million taels of gold, 50 million taels of silver, and the cession of the 3 border fortresses the Song had in the north. The emperor ordered the palace guard to search the whole city, house by house, for any valuables, put them together and handed them over to the Jurchens. They didn't even have to sack the city: the government did it for them. The Jurchens were running short of supplies, and lifted the siege in early March.

The Jurchens went home, and the Song decided to hurry and build up defenses so that they wouldn't come back again. Which sounds like the obvious thing to do. But you gotta be subtle. The Chinese were too damn obvious. First of all, the Chinese commanders in the border fortresses refused to surrender. They held up and forced the Jurchens to take over by force. The Song raised a new army and sent it up north to build up new defenses; meanwhile they sent diplomats to the remnants of the Khitan aristocracy to entice them to rebel against the Jurchens. All that in the few months after the Jurchens lifted the siege.

While the Song were obviously in a hurry to weaken the Jurchen; they just didn't understand that they were too weak for that. The Jurchen took the fortresses by force. The Khitan aristocrats weren't buying the Song offer of alliance. Those bastards! We allied with you once and you backstabbed us the moment we most needed your help. The Khitan handed the Song letter to the Jurchen emperor, which burst in rage. Those treacherous evil Chinese. These settled people have no honor. We'll show them. In October 1926 the Jurchens marched again south against China. By December they were at the gates of Kaifeng.

The Song sent armies from all across the empire to lift the siege; they were destroyed one by one. After 40 days, in February the capital of the Song Dynasty fell to the

Jurchen armies. They sacked it with abandon. Took all valuables, burnt whole quarters, raped all the women they found. They entered the palace city, and captured the whole imperial family. The emperor, Qinzong. His father, Huizong, was found on the way to his escape. All the princes, dukes, earls. Their mothers, sisters. The princesses, concubines. Everyone was taken. 15,000 people in total. Every single descendant of the second emperor, along their wives and servants was captured and sent to the Jurchen capital, one thousand miles to the north, in the freezing forests of Manchuria. Remember the climate chart? Huizong was going to live there.

Just so you get a picture of the whole thing. They went from Kaifeng to Harbin by foot. 1,500 of the prisoners died on the way. On arriving to the Jurchen headquarters, the women were auctioned by the Jurchen army. 11,000 women were taken. The emperors' wives, daughters and sisters were given as concubines to the Jurchen generals. The others, if good looking were taken to the Laundry House, the public brothel of the Jurchen state, where they were put to service the Jurchen soldiery, day and night. The servants, the children, the ugly and the old were sold as slaves in public auction. We have good records of all these because plenty of court mandarins were taken prisoner too, and they kept detailed diaries of the whole process.

So our dear emperor Huizong, the brilliant artist, the *bon vivant*, the most consummate hedonist in the history of China, ended up the prisoner of smelly barbarians in the frigid forests of Manchuria. He spent 8 long years shivering at -20C temperature, while the smelly Jurchens, who 20 years before were just a small tribe of hunter-gatherers, spit on his face and laughed at him on sight, reminding him they were fucking his wives and daughters. Huizong died a broken man in 1135. His son Qinzong was not so lucky, he lived in ignominy until 1161. He died at 51 years old, of which he spent 34 in captivity, again watching his wives, sisters and daughters ravaged by his enemies.

And so the Northern Song Dynasty was destroyed. The war continued for some years, and eventually the Jurchens conquered the whole North China plain.

The Song managed to survive in the South. Their greed took them to betray their ally of 100 years to take a small piece of land in the north. They ended up paying with the destruction and loss of half the empire, and the lives and shame of the entire imperial family. All except one single man.

The Song Dynasty's Surrender

2016-04-26 // china, history, Song Dynasty, series, power

So we left as the Jurchens conquer the Song capital of Kaifeng, empty the city of all its valuables, butcher most of the population, taking around 100,000 people as slaves. Among them the whole imperial family, 5,000 people in all, plus all their servants. The wives, mothers, sisters and daughters of the emperor and all the nobility were taken as wives, concubines, or put to work as whores in the Jurchen official brothel. Those who made it alive to the Jurchen homeland, that is. Many died on their way.

Once the Jurchen destroyed the city of Kaifeng, they grabbed one Song minister, Zhang Bangchang, gave him some of the imperial regalia they had grabbed from the Song palace, and put him as emperor of the Great Chu. Zhang was supposed to set a court at Nanjing and rule as the puppet of the Jurchens, who annexed all land north of the Yellow River, but left most Chinese territory to this puppet court. The Jurchens had no intention of ruling China at all. They had invaded to punish the Song court for its treachery and to extract some booty to share between the Jurchen generals. They achieved those goals, and then some. Setting a government in China and finding a way to rule the peasants sounded like a lot of trouble, trouble the Jurchens weren't interested in taking at all. The destruction of the Song Dynasty had also erased all public order in north China. Gangs of bandits roamed the countryside, killing landlords, public officials, Jurchen detachments and anything they could find. The Jurchen had enough men to destroy any Chinese army but it most certainly didn't have the manpower to police the whole empire. So they were happy to leave that job to that wimp Song minister, and go back home to enjoy screwing the myriad imperial princesses they had kidnapped from Kaifeng.

Mr. Zhang wasn't thrilled about this arrangement. Usurping the throne is the worst crime a Chinese minister can commit. It's tantamount to death by one thousand slices together with one's whole family. But what could he do? The entire imperial clan, thousands of men, had been taken prisoner by the Jurchens. Or not. There were rumors of a single imperial prince who was free, and had raised an army of 10,000 somewhere in the north. Prince Kang.

Huizong, our artist emperor, had had 143 wives, who had produced 38 sons and 34 daughters. Huizong didn't know them all. If Dunbar is right he barely even knew most of his women. The thing with polygamy, that some overzealous manosphere bros tend to forget, is that in traditional society sex was only allowed inside marriage. If an emperor wanted to have sex with a woman, he had to made her his concubine and take care of her for life. That means giving her proper status as the woman of that man. You can't just find her some smelly apartment in a project and give her 500 bucks alimony every month. The concubine of an emperor had to be treated as an imperial princess, and that didn't come cheap.

Prince Kang was one of the 38 sons of Huizong. In 1127, when the Jurchens invaded, he was 20 years old. He was the only child of his mother, who Huizong apparently slept with once or twice and never bother seeing again. Prince Kang though was a talented kid, tall, strong and good at the classics. But his father never met his mother, meaning his father never got to know him. The only way most Chinese emperors got to know their sons was when imperial concubines gave their pitch after having sex. "You know our son? He can write 100 letters already!" If your mother was out of favor, a prince didn't really exist. Of course he had his income as an imperial prince, and all the perks that entitled. Prince Kang at 20 years old had 4 wives, 1 son and 5 daughters.

When the Jurchens invaded China, they demanded the Song court sent an imperial prince as an envoy to discuss terms. Huizong discussed among his family, but of course nobody wanted to go. Prince Kang alone volunteered. He made quite an impression with the Jurchen generals; allegedly he was able to shot a bow so straight that the Jurchens thought the Song had tricked them. No way a

Song imperial wimp prince could shoot a bow straight, this is a fake prince! Send us a real one! Prince Kang went back home, but later was sent again as an envoy during the second invasion.

While on the road to his diplomatic mission, a regional official told Prince Kang that the Jurchens weren't joking his time, and persuaded him to abandon his mission and take refuge in the countryside. He did, but then a huge mob of local peasants came up to see what was going on. While doing so they found it was Prince Kang, alongside the Minister of War. The Minister of War yelled at them, telling them they were an imperial envoy. People found out who that guy was. They remembered it was him who had ordered to use scorched-earth tactics against the Jurchens. This guy had burnt their homes and harvests. Now he was here as a diplomatic envoy? What, he's going to sell us out to the Jurchens? The peasant mob grabbed the Minister of War of the Song Dynasty and beat him to death right there. Prince Kang, 20 years old, barely escaped with his life.

Eventually Prince Kang raised a small army, and went around avoiding the Jurchens who had just conquered the capital and taken the whole imperial clan with them; including his mother, his infant daughters and most of his wives. He only had his son and the mother of his son with him. Some time later an envoy arrives from Zhang Bangchang, the puppet minister, who wanted out of that gig and offered him the crown. So Prince Kang went over to Zhang Bangchang's fake court, and was enthroned as new emperor of the Song Dynasty, Gaozong. First order of business was to execute Zhang. He usurped the throne! Gaozong was nice and let him kill himself, and didn't punish his family.

The Jurchens, sometime after or during the wild orgies they were having with the imperial princesses up in Harbin, heard that their puppet emperor had abdicated, and that one imperial prince had escaped capture and had been enthroned as new emperor of the Song Dynasty. They were furious. They had destroyed the Song Dynasty. They had no right to start again. The Jurchens again amassed their armies and sent a massive punitive expedition, codename "Search the top of the mountains and the bottom of the sea to capture Zhao Gou (the personal name of Gaozong)". Using someone's personal name in old China is tantamount to call him a smelly bastard.

Gaozong could only flee. Flee south. He fled to the Yangtze, stayed a while in Nanjing. The Jurchen armies rushed to catch him, and he had to flee further south, to Hangzhou.

During this time there was a military coup on his side, which lasted only short while, but in the process his only son, 2 years old, died. Soon afterwards the Jurchen armies crossed the Yangtze, captured Nanjing, and were soon to get to Gaozong's court at Hangzhou. He had to get on a ship and flee south by sea. He spent weeks at sea avoiding the Jurchen armies, fleeing for his life. The whole escape was so sudden and traumatic that Gaozong had daily panic attacks. Apparently he became infertile. Traditional accounts say the Jurchen attack on Hangzhou scared him so much he became important for life. He never produced an heir.

So it's 1130 now, 3 years after the fall of Kaifeng. Eventually a Song army beat the overextended Jurchen armies, who retreated north of the Yangtze, and Gaozong returned to Hangzhou for good. He established his court there, and rebuilt the Song state apparatus in the south. Some great generals such Wu Jie, Han Shizhong and Yue Fei built strong armies who were soon able to beat the Jurchens in open battle. The Jurchens responded by retreating and setting a new puppet state in north China, headed by an old Song minister who had surrendered, Liu Yu. This guy actually liked the job, and put some effort into raising armies to fight the Song. Meanwhile the Jurchens focused on fighting in the West. China has always been unified the same way: a northern army invading Sichuan from the Xi'An area, and from there sailing down the Yangtze. The Jurchens tried hard but the Song armies held fast and blocked the Jurchen advance.

Meanwhile the Song armies were beating the puppet Chinese armies to the north. General Yue Fei was especially strong. His armies had found a way to counter the massive charges f the Jurchen heavy cavalry. He put his Chinese infantry in a sort of phalanx, with very long pikes, and had them cut the feet of the Jurchen horses as they run towards them. Now I'm simplifying a lot, but by 1140 Yue Fei was recovering more and more territory, and was close to recovering Kaifeng itself. But then his emperor Gaozong told him to stop it right there.

Gaozong had put a minister called Qin Hui as prime minister. Qin Hui had been captured by the Jurchens, and spent some time in the north. Nobody else ever escaped from capture, so there were always rumors that the Jurchens had sent him back on purpose as a spy. At any rate Gaozong was fond of the guy. Qin Hui's position was that the war was hopeless. The Song had to reach an agreement with the Jurchens and make peace as fast as possible. The Jurchen emperor had just die, and the new guy was favorable to a peace agreement. Qin Hui would make it happen as long as Gaozong gave the order.

So Yue Fei was there with his ever victorious army at the feet of Kaifeng, ready to march, when a special convoy comes directly from the court with orders to retreat, immediately. Yue Fei couldn't believe it. The work of 10 years lost in an instant! He argued once and again that they couldn't retreat, victory was at hand! But the emperor wouldn't have it. Yue Fei could only obey and resign his post.

Yue Fei is perhaps the most famous hero in Chinese history. He was the perfect man. Strong in arms, yet well educated. He was courteous, frugal, loyal and focused on his mission. He famously had a huge tattoo in his back with the letters 精忠報國, "utmost loyalty in service of the country". Mandarins from the court sent him gold, women, presents of all kind, yet he never accepted any. He had a single wife, which is unheard of in important men in China. He disciplined his army sternly and without failure, making it by far the best army in China. But he was just too perfect. In China the way to make friends with the elite is by grabbing each other's handle, sharing money, secrets, women, bad things. That way you know they will be loyal to each other; else they have something to use against you. Nobody had anything to use against Yue Fei. He was the perfect man.

That didn't save him, though. While on an audience with the emperor, Yue Fei had the nerve to ask the emperor to choose an heir. Gaozong was predisposed against the army. A military coup had killed his only son. He then became sterile, so he couldn't produce children. That indeed was a problem; what if he were to die? Yue Fei had good reason to ask him to resolve that problem. The whole imperial clan had been captured by the Jurchens, Gaozong should look for some other farther imperial relatives and create a new imperial clan. He eventually did, but that was no business of Yue Fei to ask. He was a damn general, and generals had no status in the Song Dynasty. Gaozong never forgot that slight.

Yue Fei also had the habit of saying he was fighting to expel the Jurchens from sacred Chinese territory, and push into their homeland to recover the two captured emperors. Well Gaozong wasn't very eager to recover the two captured emperors. His father made him the favor of dying in 1135, but his brother and lawful emperor was still around. The Jurchens used to threat that if the Song didn't stop winning battles, that they'd send the captured emperor on a boat straight to the new Song capital. How awkward would that be?

After Gaozong ordered Yue Fei to retreat in order to negotiate the peace treaty with the Jurchens, Qin Hui eventually trumped up charges of rebellion against Yue Fei, put him in jail and poisoned him. Other generals were furious against Qin Hui. One famously asked him:

Yue Fei was about to rebel? Nonsense! Is there any proof?!

To which Qin Hui laconically responded:

莫須有 (There doesn't need to be)

So Yue Fei, most talented, loyal and virtuous man in the empire, was killed on trumped up charges. And the Song and the Jurchen signed the peace treaty. The treaty was beyond horrible. It was the most shameful thing any Chinese dynasty had ever signed. It stipulated that the Song emperor was to refer to himself as "your servant". The Song emperor's title was to be "granted" by the Jurchens, not self-declared. The border established was also a disaster. The Song had control over much of the central plains. They could have pushed to retain the Wei river valley (the Xi'An area) and much of the central plains. But Gaozong didn't care. The border was set over the Huai river, a bit further north from the Yangtze, and that was that.

Millions of peasants who had been aiding the Song war effort were sold out and left in Jurchen territory. Many left all they had and rushed to escape into Song territory. Many didn't make it. The Jurchens didn't take it lightly.

Many wondered why the Song emperor hadn't pushed further and tried to get a better deal. In 1141 everybody understood why. The Jurchen's sent a carriage to the Song border. There was Gaozong's mother, empress Wei. While Gaozong (then prince Kang) had evaded capture, his mother, wives and daughters were taken by the Jurchens to their homeland. Gaozong's mother was 38 at the time. She was put in the Laundry House state brothel, where allegedly she was made to serve dozens of Jurchen soldiers every day. Allegedly she bore two children in the north. Gaozong had the records change to make her 10 years older, so that she would have been 48 at the time of her capture, thus officially unable of making Jurchen children. She died in 1159, officially 90 years old. Which isn't very likely. Still, living to 80 years old was quite a feat given the time, and what she had been through.

Qin Hui had secured her release by the Jurchens, in exchange of which Gaozong gave away half his empire, the best army he had, and his reputation for all posterity. Gaozong is today regarded as a despicable traitor, a coward that shamed China for centuries. Yue Fei was made a folk idol, the patron saint of all Chinese armies since. Qin Hui was made into an iron statue along his wife, which became a tourist attraction. It is customary for people to visit and spit on it.

Gaozong also lived to old age. He died in 1187, 80 years old. To choose an heir he had to find a commoner which was a descendant of the founder of the dynasty. Remember that guy[21]? The palace commander who rebelled, and then made sure his generals didn't rebel against him? His younger brother murdered him some time later. Henceforth the imperial throne was transmitted through this brother's line. Some people said that the first Jurchen emperor was the first Song emperor

---

[21] https://spandrell.ch/2016/04/19/the-distribution-of-power/

reincarnated, taking revenge on the descendants of his brother for murdering him. He certainly extinguished the whole line.

Gaozong's successor, Xiaozong tried to fix all the damage his adoptive father had done. He killed Qin Hui, repealed the peace treaty, raised armies, and tried to get back the lost territory. It didn't work. It never worked. The Jurchen ruled north China until 1234, when Genghis Khan destroyed the Jurchen state. When the Mongols started attacking north China, guess what, the Song made an alliance with them! And guess what, the Song breached the terms of the alliance, and the Mongols took that excuse to invade and destroy the Song. This time for good. To their credit the Song Dynasty held until 1279, until Genghis' grandson, Khubilai, managed to conquer them. The Mongols ruled all China for 90 years.

And that's the story of how the Song Dynasty fell and how it came back to life in the South, mostly because the emperor put more value on his mother than on 20 million of his subjects. When people like Hoppe say that Monarchs tend to govern well because they have a stake in their property, they don't know what they're talking about. Not everyone places much value on their property besides the minimum to keep their personal status. There's an old saying, which I've heard in China and Europe too: "wealth lasts but 3 generations". What the grandfather builds, the grandsons brings to the ground.

Honestly I'd probably change 20 million people for my mother, too. And I'd be glad to have a sociopath like Qin Hui to help on that. Although personally I would have done something to save my wives and daughters too. Gaozong never asked for them. 2 of his daughters survived and were married off to Jurchen men. But Chinese culture was about filial piety, children were an afterthought.

As a bonus, let me finish by telling the story of Yelu Dashi. You may have noticed that there's a light green blob in the map, way to the West of China, around what's today Xinjiang and most of Kazakhstan. You know who that is? The Khitans! The Khitan commander who held Beijing against the Song invasion, Yelu Dashi, was eventually captured by the Jurchen once they came south to help the Song out.

Yelu Dashi was not only a great general, he was a very cultivated man. He spoke Khitan and Chinese, had studied the Confucian classics, and was in charge of the administration of the Chinese areas of the Khitan empire. Shortly after he fell to the Jurchen army, Yelu Dashi escaped with his retinue. He rode fast, evading the Jurchen pursuers, and reached what's today northern Mongolia, which the Jurchen never controlled, and the Khitan had old ties of vassalage. This Khitan noblemen then raised a big army and rode to the West, conquered the Dzungar steppe, the Tarim Basin, went further West and built a huge empire that reached the Aral Sea! This new empire of Yelu ashi controlled for decades most of Central Asia, exerting its influence well into Persia. Imagine the life of this guy. He tried to raise armies to ride back east and attack the Jurchens, but it never worked out. He eventually learned to enjoy his new empire.

This new Khitan empire, called by historians the Qara-Khitai, is regarded by Chinese historians as a Chinese dynasty, the Western Liao. That's why it's painted in full color in the map. While it was a steppe empire ruled by Khitans, they kept the old Chinese-inspired administration, taught the Confucian classics, and kept many Han Chinese in the state bureaucracy. The Qara Khitai ruled Central Asia until... yes, Genghis Khan.

The Great Ming Emperor Admonishes his Troops about Women

2016-08-30

So some people are saying I'm just some rootless cosmopolitan who speaks Chinese. How can I be alt-right?

此言差矣. It doesn't work like that. I have insight precisely because I've been around, and I've read around. Let me prove my alt-right bona-fides by quoting Zhu Yuanzhang, the great founder of the Ming Dynasty, the Empire of Brightness.

Zhu Yuanzhang is the greatest rags-to-riches story in the history of mankind. He was some minor son of a landless peasant, born during the period of Mongol rule in China. Mongol government in China was quite horrible; infrastructure decayed, bandits were everywhere, and all manner of natural disasters happened all the time. One of those disasters killed our hero's whole family. Starvation. Every single one of them. Our hero had to go to the closest Buddhist temple to beg for some food; and all he got was an old wooden pan, and an order to beat the crap out of the temple and beg some food outside. Which he did for years. Beg for food. Around the country. For years. Until he met some band of bandits. Heaven had it so that his best childhood friend was a bandit chief; so he soon joined them. Our hero then slowly but steadily climbed the bandit meritocracy ladder; next thing you know he is leading the best rebel army in China, expels the Mongols to the steppe and reunifies All Under Heaven.

There's something to say for the tradition, the slow accumulation of knowledge in society. But some things just don't require an education. Just razor-sharp smarts. And industrial amounts of cruelty. And Zhu Yuanzhang had those. He was an illiterate beggar, and yet he built and commanded the armies that beat the Mongols and founded the Ming Dynasty. Not unlike Genghis Khan; he also didn't need to go to school to command the best run armies in the history of mankind. Politics really isn't that hard.

Anyway, one of the most fun things of the founder of the Ming is that he was illiterate. Which in China is a problem, as elite people were supposed to be able to write in Classical Chinese, which is kinda like Latin in the West. Obviously he couldn't do that, so many of his edicts are written in plain vernacular language. So he would sent imperial decrees to his troops saying "grab those damn Japanese pirates and slit their fucking throats on the spot. This is My Command". He was very fond of sending commands, edicts and decrees to the whole country. China is a big country; and the guy, for all his illiteracy, had many ideas. He had built and run the army who conquered the country. Surely running the country in peace couldn't be that hard? All you need is order and discipline. And he knew something about that.

Anyway, this is one small snippet of his views on women and sexual propriety:

男子婦人必要有分別。婦人家專一在裡面，不可外出來。若露頭露臉出外來呵，必然有惹淫亂的事。而今有等愚夫愚婦好生部不守道理，把風俗壞了。便如曲靖衛指揮牛麟，他在雲南討一個婦人做妾，每日與同僚官喫酒，便着這婦人出來同座喫酒。因此上被指揮柳英誘引私通，教本婦將毒藥毒死牛麟。有這等無知的，婦人家如何着他與男子漢喫酒，喫一會酒了，自家的性命也被人害了。若是有分別呵，那裡有這等事。指揮柳英與那婦人，都將殺了。今後再有這等的，拿住一般罪他。

Which translates as:

There must be a separation between men and women. Women must be always inside the house, must not be allowed to come outside. If they go out of the home revealing their head or their face, that will inevitably result in lewdness and debauchery. But these days there are some stupid men and stupid women who can't reason properly and make a mess of proper morality.

See for example this the Commander of Qujing, this Niu Lin guy. While he was in Yunnan he got some woman as a concubine, and when he went to drink with his comrades, he would take her to drink with them! So of course she ended up being seduced by another commander called Liu Ying, who then had her poison her husband Niu Lin.

Just how dumb was this guy? He brought his wife to drink with other men, drunk for a while, next thing you know he got killed. If he had kept a proper separation between men and women, nothing like this could have happened. I had Liu Ying and that woman killed. If something like this ever happens again, they'll get the same treatment.

The 36 Stratagems

There's always a way

2021-1-12

There's a nifty book in China called the 三十六計. The "36 stratagems". Nobody knows when the book was written, though it must be old, the first mention of it goes back to the 5th century AD, when it was attributed to Tan Daoji 譚道濟, a general for the Liu Song Dynasty. The consensus is that he did indeed write it.

The 36 stratagems are organized as six different scenarios, with six stratagems each. Each stratagem is phrased as a catchy four letter idiom, the staple of Chinese vocabulary, and most of them have since become common idioms known even by small children. The book also quotes extensively the Yijing 易經, the Book of Changes, the famous book on divination. For no good reason really, but it does sound cool.

The six scenarios vary on the balance of power they apply to. Generally speaking half the stratagems apply to when you have an advantage in the war, when you are stronger than your enemy, while the other half are for when you are in a weaker position.

The last scenario is outright called 敗戦計 "tactics for when you're losing the war", and describe crafty attempts to gain an advantage or reverse the course of the fight. You may not be able to fight your enemy head on in the open, but that doesn't mean there's nothing you can do. There's plenty of tactics that a committed force can use even when fighting a vastly stronger enemy.

For no reason in particular, certainly nothing to do with current events, I am going to make a series of posts translating the last 6 stratagems in the book, those to be used when you're losing the war. Interestingly the 6 last stratagems are the only ones not phrased as with 4-letter idioms. They are instead titled with two letters each, with the last one being three. I guess the author wanted to make the point that when you're losing the war you have no time for florid language and witty metaphors: just get to the fucking point.

And that he did. I'll translate the very last stratagem, also the most famous during the ages, being quoted in many pieces of literature since the book was written 1600 years ago.

On the translation: First line is the name of the stratagem. Second line is the original text, purportedly going back to the 5th century. Then comes the "按語", an elaboration written much later, probably in the mid Ming (15-16th century). I like my translations as literal as possible.

走為上

To run is best.

全師避敵 左次無咎 未失常也

Avoid the enemy with all your troops. There is no fault in retreat, no loss of normality in it.

敵勢全勝，我不能戰，則必降，必和，必走。降則全敗，和則半敗，走則未敗，未敗者，勝之轉機也。

如宋畢再遇與金人對壘，度金兵至者日眾，難與爭鋒。一夕拔營去，留旗幟與營，豫縛生羊懸之，置其前二足於鼓上，羊不堪倒懸，則足擊鼓有聲。金人不覺，相持數日，始覺之，欲追之，則已遠矣，可謂善走者矣。

If the enemy is achieving total victory, and we are unable to fight, one must surrender, make peace, or run. Surrender means complete defeat. Peace means half defeat. Running means no defeat. To be undefeated can be turned into victory.

Like the Song dynasty general Bi Zaiyu, who fighting the Jurchens, realized the Jurchen army was growing stronger every day and he couldn't compete. One evening he dismantled his camp, leaving his army banner in place, then got a sheep and hanged it from a rope, so that its front legs would be on top of an army drum. The sheep, distressed at hanging in the air, would hit the drums with its legs and make them sound [TN: as if the troops were still around]. The Jurchens didn't realize what was happening, waited in place for days until they finally noticed the retreat. They wanted to pursue the Song army but it had run too far by then. We can say he did well by running.

That's it for now, more stratagems to come later this week.

The Honeypot

2021-1-21

Biden was inaugurated yesterday. Didn't watch the thing, it's kinda depressing, so I went back to my old disinterested, cynical self. I used to be very happy ignoring mainstream politics. Damn you, Trump, you pulled me out of my detached cool lifestyle. Well it was more the pepes and other 4chan memes created since 2016. Damn you guys. I used to not care. I didn't want to care. But you draw me in. It was great. I had a lot of fun. But it was wrong. We all knew it was wrong, that it wouldn't get anywhere. And yet... Oh well. What is done is done.

Now back to regular programming. As promised I'll go with my translation of the 三十六計, the 36 stratagems of ancient Chinese warfare. Well, I'm only translating six stratagems, the six stratagems to use when you're in the weak side, losing the war against a strong enemy. Last time I did the very last one, which can be summarized as gtfo. Today it's turn for Stratagem #31.

美人計

The Honeypot

(literally: The Beautiful Person Trick)

兵強者，攻其將。將智者，伐其情。將弱兵強，其勢自萎。利用禦寇，順相保也。

When the enemy army is strong, attack its commander. When the commander is smart, attack his emotions. When the troops are strong but their commander is weak, its momentum withers on its own. Use this to resist your enemy and you will protect yourself successfully.

兵強將智，不可以敵，勢必事之。事之以土地，以增其勢，如六國之事秦，策之最下者也。事之以幣帛，以增其富，如宋之事遼金，策之下者也。惟事之以美人，以佚其志，以弱其體，以增其下之怨，如勾踐以西施重寶取悅吳王夫差，乃可轉敗為勝。

When the enemy army is strong and its commanders are intelligent, you just can't compete, you have to surrender something.

If you give them land, it increases the enemy's power. That's what happened to the six states and Qin [which eventually destroyed them and founded the first Empire]. That's the worst possible tactic. If you give the money and silk, it increases the enemy's wealth. That's what happened with the Song Dynasty vs. the Khitans and Jurchens. Also a bad tactic. The only good tactic is to give them hot chicks. That shaves away theirs resolve, weakens their bodies and increases the resentment of their subordinates. That's what happened with Gou Jian, King of Yue, who sent Xi Shi [legendary beauty in China to this day] to Fu Chai, King of Wu. That's the way to turn defeat into victory.

My book has some extra examples for illustration, let me introduce a funny one:

During the An Lushan rebellion, Tang Dynasty general Li Guangbi was sent to resist [An Lushan's second in command and later successor] the rebel armies of Shi Siming. The two armies soon found each other and dug trenches across a river and the situation stagnated.

At the time Shi Siming's army was slightly stronger than Li Guangbi's, having more than 1,000 high quality war horses. One day Shi Siming ordered a subordinate to take their thousand hourses to the river to drink and wash, but actually he just wanted to show them off to intimidate the governmenet forces. Li Guangbi heard of this and thought of a trick. He sent a subordinate to gather every single mare in his army, a total of around 500, and sent them close to the river where the rebel army's horses were drinking.

The mares started crying and moving excitedly as they approached the 1,000 war horses of the rebel army, and those horses on seeing the mares run straight away towards them, crossing the river and leaving their soldiers behind.

Thus, the government forces easily captured 1,000 strong war horses, and the rebel armies had to retreat several miles after losing much of its military advantage.

Commentary:

This might seem quite irrelevant for my readership and current affairs. Honeypots are indeed old as sin, and quite effective. And they don't require strong armies so they can be used by people in a weak position in order to gain some advantage.

But they're also not a trick which is exclusive to people in a weak position. Honeypots are just as powerful when used from a position of strength. Governments, police forces use honeypots all the time to capture criminals or dissidents. It's just a good and rather cheap trick no matter who initiates it.

If anything, I think you could say that using women against their enemies is a trick that the left has been using a lot. For centuries really. To a large extent the victory of leftism against traditional society, since the very beginning really, has been a long, centuries-long, sustained honeypot. Not just sending hot chicks to get some short term advantage or extract some incel. It's a rather more insidious sort: it's using all our women, our wives, our sisters, our daughters! in a life-long mission to sow discord and division among our ranks. The mother of all honeypots.

What to do? Write your suggestions in the comments.

By the way my call to people to join my Urbit group has been massively successful. ~docteg-mothep/bloody-shovel is right now the most active group on Urbit! You're missing out. This post will be published there too, do come and join the discussion.

The Empty Fortress

2021-1-25 // china, history, war

Today it's Stratagem 32:

The Empty Fortress

虛者虛之，疑中生疑，剛柔之際，奇而複奇。
Those who are empty, empty it. Create uncertainty inside uncertainty. Between hard and soft, be strange and strange again.

虛虛實實，兵無常勢。虛而示虛，諸葛而後，不乏其人。

如吐蕃陷瓜州，王君煥死，河西恟懼。以張守珪為瓜州刺史，領餘眾方複築州城。版乾裁立，敵又暴至。略無守禦之具，城中相顧失色，莫有鬥志。守珪曰："徒眾我寡，又瘡痍之後，不可以矢石相持，須以權道制之。"乃於城上，置酒作樂，以會將士。敵疑城中有備，不敢攻而退。 又如齊祖珽為北徐州刺史。至州，會有陳寇，百姓多反。珽不關城門。守陴者皆令下城，靜坐街巷，禁斷行人，雞犬不亂鳴吠。賊無所見聞，不測所以，或疑人走城空，不設警備。珽複令大叫，鼓譟聒天，賊大驚，登時走散。

Empty or full [weak or strong], there are no constants in warfare. Of weak armies who show openly their weakness, ever since Zhuge Liang, there have been many.

For example when the Tibetans conquered Guazhou [in 776], Wang Junhuan died, and the West edges of the Yellow River all fell into panic. Zhang Shougui, governor of Guazhou, took the remainer population and started to build a new fortress. With the scaffolding for the walls was just finished the enemy attached again.

They had no means of defense, and everyone immediately turned pale, with no will to fight. Wang then gave a speech: "The enemy are many, and we are few. We've just survived a defeat, we can't fight again with arrows and stones, we must use other means to defeat them". Saying this he went to the top of the fortress, served some wine, played some music, and held a banquet with his soldiers. The enemy on seeing this thought the fortress was well prepared, so they retreated.

Or like Zu Ting of the Northern Qi, governor of Xuzhou. On arriving to his post, he found enemy troops from the Chen Dynasty, and many peasant rebellions. Zu ordered to let the city gates unshut, and have all the defendors go downtown and sit quietly in the alleys, while forbidding people from walking around and making sure roosters and dogs made no noise. When the enemy arrived they saw the open gates but nobody in the streets, not knowing why, with some suspecting perhaps everyone had left and the city was empty and undefended. At that moment Zu loudly shouted commands, the war drums blasted their sound up to heaven. The enemies, frightened, scattered away immediately.

Commentary: This is a bit of a stretched metaphor, but in a sense we're already running an empty fortress trick, and we have for a long time. Just that it's not we running the trick, but us being forced to.

The Left is strong and has dominated most wings of government for centuries. Their rhetoric however makes them repeat the mantra that they are the underdog, the weak and vulnerable, while the right is this scary mass of violent power, eager to attack them at any time.

In ancient war, the most important thing was discipline. If an army kept formation and obeyed orders, 9 times out of 10 they were pretty much invincible. Most deaths were not during battles, but after one side had lost cohesion and scattered troops could be hunted down easily by the victors. In that circumstance numbers didn't really matter. Scattered troops running away are useless, whether there's one thousand of one million of them.

Hence the scariest thing for an army commander was being ambushed and caught by surprise. Showing yourself to the enemy to be too weak just doesn't make sense: you're basically begging them to attack and kill you. The only rational explanation is that it's a trap, and traps are dangerous. So it's a neat trick to use, assuming the enemy doesn't have good information of your strength, and you have the massive balls to pull it off.

Does the Left have good information on the Right's strength? They surely have, but can they use it? The truth is highly inconvenient for them. They're always pretending that any affront on the right will unleash a "violent backlash" by the fierce right wing masses. Which don't really exist anymore. But they need them to exist. So the Right is kept alive, barely, left to exist not because of mercy, but to be forced to play a part in the Left's running LARP.

Sow Distrust, and Profit

2021-2-13 // history, china, loyalty

Time for our next stratagem, the 反間計.

It's rather hard to translate the name itself. Literally it's "counter-between". A "between" is what foreign agents were called in ancient China. Half spies, half agents to sow discord in the enemy ranks.

Original text and translation follows:

疑中之疑比之自內不自失也

Doubts inside doubts. Befriend from the inside, you won't lose.

間者使敵自相疑忌也 反間者因敵之間而間之也

Secret agents [lit. "betweens"] spread doubt within your enemy. Counter-agents do that to your enemy's own agents.

如燕昭王薨，惠王自為太子時，不快於樂毅。 田單乃縱反間曰： 樂毅與燕王有隙，畏誅，欲連兵王齊。 齊人未附故且緩攻即墨，以待其事。齊人唯恐他將來，即墨殘矣。 惠王聞之，即使騎劫代將，毅遂奔趙。

When King Zhao of Yan died, King Hui took the throne. He didn't like General Yue Yi ever since he was crown prince. Tian Dan [general of Qi during a massive war with Yan], unleashed a counter-op, saying: "Yue Yi doesn't have a good relation with his King, and fears he might be executed. He's thinking on bringing his trips and install himself as King at Qi. The people at Qi haven't committed to him yet which is why he's delaying his attack on Jimo [a city of Qi he was besieging]. The people of Qi are most afraid of Yue Yi being replaced by some other general, as then Jimo will certainly be sacked." King Hui of Yan heard of this story, immediately sent Qi Jie to replace Yue Yi, and Yue Yi fled to Zhao.

又如周瑜利用曹操間諜，以間其將。陳平以金縱反間於楚軍，間范增，楚王疑而去之。亦疑中之疑之局也。

Or like Zhou Yu [famous general of the state of Wu during the Three Kingdoms period] fooled an undercover agent sent by Cao Cao to mislead his general. Or Chen Ping, using money to spread doubts on the Chu Army, making it look as if Fan Zeng was disloyal. The King of Chu grew suspicious and removed him. All these were tricks to spread doubts inside doubts.

Commentary:

This is one of the classics, used very, very often in history, often with great success.

The strongest thing in the world is a cohesive army of men who trust each other and have a common purpose. They can literally achieve anything they work on. Make them distrust each other, though, and no matter how numerous, how strong, how wealthy or how technically advanced, they just lose the ability to project power effectively. You can't get anything done if you're afraid your underlings (or your superiors!) are going to stab in your sleep. Any human organization runs on trust. It follows that to win, you must undermine the trust among your enemies. Especially if you're in a position of weakness.

Of course that assumes a flat, meritocatic scenario with a lot of mobility, which was often the case in China, or in the Roman Empire, up onto the very end of Constantinople plagued with dissension and betrayals and all sorts of stratagems. European or Japanese warfare was less afflicted by that because feudalism is quite good at enforcing loyalty, and in Europe warfare often had ethnic or religious background to it.

Well, do we live today in a feudal, fragmented society, or a global meritocracy? You might see now why I write about Chinese history so much. It's not just that I like it, it's actually much more relevant than you'd think.

Now, the stratagem above and their examples give the general idea of the counter-op. But there is a variant of this strategy not detailed in this collection, a variant which

I find of the utmost importance. It is much more insidious, but so much more effective. It's the counter-op on steroids. The mother of all counter-ops.

Let's talk about Ying Bu 英布. Also known as Qing Bu 黥布, i.e. Bu the Tattooed. More on that soon.

The time is 209 BC. The Qin Dynasty, the First Empire, has collapsed after only 12 years, as the death of the first emperor ignited a palace crisis and the whole country, nostalgic of their recently vanquished kingdoms, rose in rebellion against the heavy handed rule of the Qin. The Qin dynasty was known to history as following the ideology of Legalism, an idea of government through clear laws of rewards and punishment, strictly applied, with no loopholes or privileges. Confucians, who eventually became the mainstream ideology in China, always refer to Legalism as cruel and inhuman. What they don't say is that Legalism works, and is almost wholly responsible for the rise of the state of Qin from frontier backwater to the founder of the First Empire.

Sometimes Legalist do over do it, however, and the early Qin empire was famously harsh with their punishments. They might have felt that it was necessary in order to tame a recently conquered massive population, but they certainly overdid it. They had two basic problems: one was the overly wide use of the death penalty. The death penalty is important to remove shitty people from the population. But you must only use it to punish the worst crimes of all, basically murder and extreme cruelty; else you're pushing lighter criminals into murder. If you punish rape with death, rapists might as well kill their victims too.

Well, the early Qin famously punished arriving late to a military commission with death. And so Chen Sheng and Wu Guang got bogged down by torrential rains in Dazexiang, and knew they would be killed for it, they famously said: 等死，死國可乎 "If we're dying anyway, might as well die for our [old] country". And so they rose in rebellion and proclaimed the restoration of the State of Chu.

Second problem with the harsh criminal laws of the early Qin was that any man with a slightly above average level of testosterone was likely to see himself in the wrong side of the law; and the relentless, thorough Qin legal machinery would see him branded for life (an old Chinese punishment is tattooing the word "criminal" in the forehead) and sent to hard labor. Hard labor sucks, but if you have a bunch of big, strong guys, branded for life, expelled for good from polite society; well you better make sure that this relentless state machinery is kept well oiled and stable all times. Because if it's not, at the slightest show of unrest, these guys are not an embryonic army. They're an army alright.

So this takes us to Ying Bu. Ying Bu was a big, tall, strong guy, who for some probably violent crime got tattooed in the face and sent to build Qin Shihuang's mausoleum at Lishan. There he was, shoveling earth around with a bunch of several thousand big, tall, strong, violent tatted bros when news come that there's a bunch of big rebellions all over the place and the government is basically not functioning anymore.

Ying Bu naturally decides that he wants a piece of the action, so he raises a gang with his fellow prisoner bros and goes around robbing caravans, stealing women, claiming territory and raising more troops. Good times.

Soon Ying Bu was commanding a few thousand men, and as it happened, he was a masterful commander and brave warrior, winning a series of battles against government troops. As the civil war progressed, Ying Bu was persuaded to join the, at the moment, largest army of all, that of Xiang Yu, who controlled the heir of the house of Chu, the largest of the pre-unification kingdoms. Ying Bu again showed himself to be a brilliant commander and was made a nobleman of the kingdom of Chu. In 207 at the great battle of Julu, the Chu armies destroyed the main force of the Qin Dynasty, a battle in which Ying Bu had a decisive role to play, holding the flank of his army against superior government forces.

After the battle of Julu, Xiang Yu went around burying alive hundreds of thousands of Qin troops, mopping up any opposition he found, and triumphantly conquering the Qin capital at Xianyang, which he burnt to the ground, no fucks given. The amount of ancient treasure and literature that was lost at the time, I shudder to think. Oh well. The wages of war.

Soon after his triumphant tour, Xiang Yu, now basically lord of the realm, decided he just wanted to grill. He had Ying Bu kill the King of Chu he supposedly served, put himself as King of Western Chu, and divided the rest of the country among his underlings, 18 of them. Among them obviously was Ying Bu, his loyal general, always at his side leading the shock troops, doing the dirty and dangerous work while Xiang Yu stayed at the rear. Ying Bu was made King of Jiujiang, just south of Xiang's own territory. From mutilated prisoner to King, Ying Bu had gone a long way. Good times. Very good times.

But of course it didn't end that way. Everybody in China knows about Xiang Yu, but what they know about Xiang Yu is how dumb he was. First, don't fucking burn the capital, there's good stuff there. Second, once you burn the capital don't fucking go home and retire. What the hell. How is dividing the country randomly in 19 pieces to random dudes who 10 years before were mutilated prisoners working hard labor sentences going to be a stable arrangement. It almost immediately broke down, as Liu Bang, just made King of Han, decided he wanted a bigger piece of the pie.

The rest is history, as Chinese people today are known as Han, so called because of the Han Dynasty, so called because Liu Bang conquered the country as King of Han, a title given to him by Xiang Yu during that weird 19-fold division of the country when he retired home to grill in 206 BC. So yes, that guy won, and Xiang Yu got wrecked, little by little, for a long 4 years. Poor guy didn't see it coming. But he should.

So Liu Bang eventually conquered the whole thing, the 19 statelets. So what happened to Ying Bu? Was he killed defending his little kingdom of Jiujiang? Oh no, this is where it gets interesting. So this is the thing, Liu Bang was no strong, 7 foot chad warrior. He was a rather short, scrawny, cowardly guy. But he was smart, and most importantly, he was both evil and nice, and had exquisite timing on when to be which. Liu Bang famously said that he didn't have any talents, but that he got so far in life (the guy was a village drunkard before he became Emperor of one of the largest empires known to man) because he had good friends. And that's indeed the most important talent in life: how to make useful friends.

Well Ying Bu was a useful friend to have, obviously. One of the best military minds (and bodies) in the world. But at this point (206 BC, Liu Bang attacks Xiang Yu), Ying Bu was not Liu Bang's friend. He was Xiang Yu's friend, the other guy's friend. What's to be done? Well Liu Bang had to turn the guy. Not easy though, Ying Bu had been one Xiang Yu's right hand man for years, accompanying him around in almost every campaign, and even killing the nominal emperor (the erstwhile King of Chu; long story) for him.

But he was now king for his realm, and after a couple years of kingship, Ying Bu had grown a bit lazy. Several times his erstwhile big brother Xiang Yu had asked him to raise troops and help him in his campaigns, but Ying Bu claimed he was sick and refused to go out. For all we know he was actually sick, but Xiang Yu wasn't happy about it, and people who angered Xiang Yu had a tendency to ended up stabbed and thrown in a ditch. At any rate there was a civil war going on and Ying Bu had perfectly good reasons to not commit on either side just yet. The smart play was obviously to let other people fight it out, conserve your strength, and then sweep them both, with a bit of luck maybe pull a Muhammad against Persia and Byzantium.

That was not to happen though, as Liu Bang was just too crafty. He sent an envoy to Ying Bu, telling him Xiang Yu is cringe, everybody hates him, Han is taking him down any day now, might as well join the party now while the going is early and we're feeling generous. We'll give you a bigger patch of land or something. Ying Bu remained uncommitted, reasonably taking his time to think about it. But the Han army was not going to give him that time. On seeing that a Xiang Yu envoy was meeting Ying Bu, Liu Bang's envoy rushed in uninvited, pushed away the guards and just yelled: "Ying Bu is with us now! Why the hell would he send troops to help Xiang Yu!".

Ying Bu was aghast. That fucking Han envoy had slandered him in public in front of the one guy who could and most certainly will kill him if he got suspicious of defection. Xiang Yu didn't joke around. He didn't need proof. He just got angry and killed people all the time.

You can imagine the Han envoy, giggling, wispering at his ear. "Well, if that's the case... you might as well, like, do it. Kill Xiang Yu's envoy, rally your troops, and come join the Han army. Come on, you'll like it there. We'll treat you well."

And so Ying Bu was very much forced to take sides in favor of Liu Bang. He killed Xiang Yu's envoy, left his fief, and run to the Han camp. He was soon made a great general of a big Han army and after the final victory he was made King again of a slightly bigger kingdom. So it all turned alright (well, not in the very end, but that's another story).

But the fact is Ying Bu didn't take sides himself. He was forced to. By an ally, a guy who needed him and treated him well. But he had to be forced to defect. And by forcing Ying Bu to defect, Liu Bang didn't only sow discord and perhaps deprive his enemy of one of his best generals, which is the basic idea of the stratagem. He deprived his enemy of a good general *and* obtained the general for himself. Genius.

If you still don't get it, I'll elaborate on lesson of this story on the next post.

The Self Harming Trick

2021-3-4

Hi, welcome back to our series on Ancient Chinese War Stratagems.

Today we will translate stratagem 34. 苦肉計, the Self Harming Trick.

人不自害 受害必真 假真真假 間以得行 童蒙之吉 順以巽也

People don't hurt themselves. If they are hurt, it must be true. Fake the true, true the fake, between and you will succeed. It is auspicious that children are ignorant, as they can be thus molded.

間者，使敵人相疑也；反間者，因敵人之疑，而實其疑也；苦肉計者，蓋假作自間以間人也。凡遣與己有隙者以誘敵人，約為響應，或約為共力者，皆苦肉計之類也。如：鄭武公伐胡而先以女妻胡君，並戮關其思；韓信下齊而驪生遭烹。

Betweens cause the enemy to suspect themselves, counter-betweens make those suspicions of the enemy become real. The Self-harming trick is sort of like running a fake op on yourself in order to run a real op on your enemy. Self-harming tricks make it look like there's a gap in your own line in order to lure the enemy in, promise him you will undermine your own side for him, or at least help him. As when Duke Wu of Zheng 鄭武公 who before attacking the state of Hu 胡, gave a daughter in marriage to the lord of Hu and killed a minister who argued for attacking them. Or when Han Xin 韓信 attacked the state of Qi 齊 and Li Shiqi 酈食其 got boiled alive.

Commentary:

Well this is an odd one, but the idea is clear. You need to fool the enemy, distract him, get his attention off you somehow. A way of doing that might be to harm yourself in order to feign weakness; feign so much weakness that the enemy stops bothering to attack you. Then you attack.

You might call this the Art of War version of being passive-aggressive.

As I said recently Scott Alexander shutting down his blog in reaction to the New York Times announcing they would dox him was a sort of Self Harming Trick. Sort of like a crazy girlfriend saying she'd kill herself if you flirt with the waitress. Signals earnestness. But again, people never harm themselves, if they do, it's always a trick. Now you know.

Bureaucracy & Monarchy

The Chinese Bureaucracy, 1

2014-01-07

Don't believe the hype: learning Chinese is hard. Very hard. It's not for every one. Pronunciation is hard, grammar isn't as easy as often said, characters are insane, and every city has its own dialect or outright different language which makes it very hard to understand anything unless people actually want you to understand.

And what makes it harder of all is that there's just so little interesting content in Mandarin. I know people who learned German to read Schopenhauer. Schopenhauer himself is said to have learned Spanish in his old age to be able to read Calderón de la Barca's plays. Manga and videogames have motivated many to learn Japanese.

But what do you learn Mandarin with? Mandarin prose itself is quite recent, with 18th century Dream of the Red Chamber becoming an unofficial standard, which saw an explosion of creativity in the Republican era. But the Communists killed that movement right after assuming power in 1949, so the only decent literature in Mandarin is all compressed in about 30 years. Taiwan and Hong Kong have not picked up the slack, so decent content in

Mandarin pretty much died. And it can barely be said to have recovered by now, even after 30 years of opening.

I eventually found my killer app (TV soap operas and Wang Shuo), and through them developed a deep appreciation towards the Beijing dialect. It has a bad rep with Chinese intellectuals for having a Manchu superstrate and being a language of idle vagrants and swindlers who can't stop talk. But that's the beauty of it, Beijing people talk a lot, talk fast, and they constantly spout classical idioms one after the other to compete on awesomeness.

Still, not living there and having more or less consumed all the decent content that I could found (content from the last 10 years has declined precipitously in quality), my Chinese had started to falter again. So I was extremely happy to find a new killer app with which to practice, one that also suited my more adult intellectual leanings. I found Yuan Tengfei[22]. My Mandarin has improved 1 year worth of practice just by watching his clips for a week.

Mr. Yuan is a high school history professor in Beijing. He got famous when recordings of his classes went viral online. First because he's hilarious and awesome at the same time. He explains Chinese and World history with superb detail while translating it to colloquial and

---

[22] https://www.youtube.com/user/yuantengfeinet

humorous Beijing vernacular. And he is also opinionated and outspoken. His popularity went out of the roof when his lectures on the Mao Zedong era went public, where he openly calls Mao a murderous butcher, who has killed more Chinese than all foreign devils combined.

You'd think they'd grabbed the guy and sent him to a Gulag for good. For a while he went silent, and we all thought the worse. But not long later the guy came back, and on national TV! Saner minds prevailed and now the guy has his own show on national TV. And you can see he's not having a hard time; since he got his new gig he's gained at least 30 pounds.

He has more than a thousand videos in his Youtube channel, so there's enough material there to keep you busy for years. I'll like to show one of his most recent pieces, in which he briefly explains how life was the people in the power structure in Imperial China.

So let me translate the first clip: Chancellors.[23]

Today we're going to talk about how stressful is the life of a Chancellor.

The job of a Chancellor ain't easy. Why? Well because in Ancient Despotism, the state is a family state. Who owns the state? The Emperor's family. And that's why the

---

[23] https://www.youtube.com/watch?v=iJUO3bzGx5M

Emperor's job is how to make sure he doesn't lose his family's estate.

The Emperor has to detect all potential threats to his rule, and cut them before they get big. Why are Chancellors a threat to Emperors? The position of Chancellor was started by the First Emperor of Qin after unifying China. The Han Dynasty also kept the Qin system in place. According to the history books, the job of the Chancellor was to assist the Emperor and help him in all matters. He's in charge of everything!

And in the Qin and Han dynasties, there's only one Chancellor, so he had a lot of power. He had the right to dismiss Imperial edicts! If the Chancellor didn't agree with an Imperial edict, say he grabs the scroll and says: "Nope, I don't agree with this". He rolls back again and returns it. And he could also write his own opinions on the back of the scroll. Say, he gets a scroll and writes: "We need to have public healthcare, and the state should pay for old-age pensions. It's not good that only civil servants have health insurance, the people might revolt." So they got the scroll, write their own opinions and returned it to the Emperor.

Generally whatever the Chancellor decided had to be done, was done. And when the Chancellor went to court, like when the Emperor publishes his edicts in front of everyone, well then it's just awesome. If you've seen the movie "Red Cliff", when Cao Cao meets the Emperor, that's quite accurate. The Chancellor had 3 privileges. He could carry a sword in court and wear shoes. Before the Tang Dynasty, people in China sit on the floor like the Koreans and Japanese today. The floor was covered by mats, so you had to take your shoes off. But the Chancellor didn't; he wore his shoes and carry his sword.

Second privilege is the Chancellor doesn't bow. The Emperor sits on his throne, everyone else is bowing down like this, but the Chancellor doesn't need to bow. He can walk with swag. And the third privilege: he doesn't call his own name. The ancient Chinese called their own name as a way of showing humility. You used your name with your teachers, your parents, with your boss. But if you call me by my name I'd beat you up. Won't talk to you ever again. You can't call me by my name, you have to use my courtesy name.

So most people when talking to the Emperor would use their own names, but the Chancellor doesn't. He refers to himself as "minister", and that's it. That's his special treatment. So the Chancellor had all this power, and this elevated treatment, so of course there were many "power Chancellors", Chancellors who just want to grab power. Everybody knows the famous ones, Wang Mang, Cao Cao. Later during the Southern and Northern dynasties, it was insane. Every Chancellor out there was usurping the throne. If you were a Chancellor and didn't grab the throne for yourself, the commoners would get worried.

"What, no change of Dynasty yet? Come on, just do it, with a new Dynasty our salaries might rise, taxes can fall, at least an amnesty, right?"

So that's why at the end of the Southern and Northern dynasties, the last usurper of all, Yang Jian, who was the maternal grandfather of the Northern Zhou Emperor, took the throne for himself and established the Sui Dynasty. Afterwards Yang Jian thought to himself: "Why did I get to be Emperor? Because I was the Chancellor. I had a lot of power. So we must make sure that this doesn't happen again to my descendants. How? Well the problem is there's only one Chancellor. So I'll make a whole bunch of them. This way they can check and balance each other."

And so he divided the government in three departments: the Chancellery. the Secretariat, and State Affairs. The chiefs and vice-chiefs of every department all had the treatment of Chancellor. Each department had a chief and 2 vice-chiefs, so 3 by 3, 9 Chancellors. Now the power of the Chancellors was scattered, so no chance of a rebellion. One Chancellor had become a bunch of them.

Later during the Song Dynasty, the Emperor started to think again. Yes we changed one Chancellor into a bunch, but they still have a lot of power. Why? Because they handle everything. Hop on a horse, lead the army, hop down form a horse, they lead the people. Generals outside, ministers inside. They also directed the wars! The cabinet is leading the army. That's no good. So I'll grab the most important powers, the military and the treasury, and take them away from the Chancellors. So we set a Ministry of Defence, and a Treasury Department, so the Chancellors can't lead an army, and don't have access to the Treasury either.

First the Chancellor was made into a bunch, then they took away the military and the money; so they had little left. That's how little by little, the threat that the Chancellors represented decreased until they could never threaten anyone again. This system was already very good, but...

The Ming Dynasty founder, the Hongwu Emperor came up. Zhu Yuanzhang [his name], where'd he come from? Even worse than Liu Bang, at least Liu Bang had been a street patrol officer. But Zhu Yuanzhang during the previous Dynasty was a beggar! His name was Zhu Double Eight, his father was Zhu Five Four! His grandpa was Zhu New Year. Hear those names and you know what kind of cultural level the family had. So this man had come from the very lowest rung of society, up into heaven. This kind of man values extremely highly the power he has grabbed in his hands. It didn't come easily.

So aren't the Chancellors the biggest threat to the Emperor? OK, abolished, get out. During the Ming and Qing dynasties, there were no Chancellors. The Emperor assumed the office themselves. "I'm the Chancellor. All power in one person, I lord over my ministers." Thing is this little fucker got exhausted. 300 issues to deal with every day. Do the math. So when some scroll came to court which was too long, he'd just beat the author. Thing he's just too busy, can't listen to everything. One time this official sent a scroll 17,000 letters long. "Who the hell do you think I am, is this a fucking novel or what. Beat him! So they started beating the poor guy while the Emperor listened to the text, which made a lot of sense actually. So after a while the Emperor called for the guy to be brought up, but they'd already wasted him.

Zhu Yuanzhang was so damn twisted, he didn't trust anyone. He was exhausted. He'd want everyone to stay put, nicely obedient, so everything would be easy. So he set up a spy operation, to spy on his ministers. They watched everything. One example: there was this official at the Ministry of Personnel, called Qian. One day the Emperor called him to court, and asked him: "What did you do yesterday night?".

Qian answered that with he was playing cards with some colleagues.

"Cards huh. Who were you playing with?"

"Some colleagues, Mr. Yang, Mr. Sun, Mr. Yu, playing the 4 of us."

"So who won then?"

"Thing is we were playing but then we realized that we were missing one card, so we couldn't go on playing."

Zhu Yuanzhang nodded, and said "Good, you're an honest man." Then he reached into his sleeve and took a playing card. "Is this the card you were missing?"

This was the middle of winter, but little Qian's sweat was pouring out of his clothes. Now you don't know which of the three playing pals is a spy! If during yesterday's game someone said something critical of the Emperor, you're a dead man.

So one of the tragedies of Chinese history is that the power of the Emperor constantly grew, while the power of the ministers constantly fell. Before the Song dynasty, the ministers discussed all matters together, and ruled as a group. But during the Yuan, Ming and Qing dynasties, autocracy become stronger, and the relation between the Ruler and his ministers became that of an Owner and his slaves.

When you watch historical soap operas, you can see He Shen (a famous Manchu minister in the Qing Dynasty), shouting when meeting the emperor: "Your Slave Heshen is here". Such an important official, but he was still a slave.

So why did China fall into this tragedy? Perhaps it has to do with the ever tighter Autocratic system.

It's interesting that European history is often taught as a linear narrative where autocracy little by little gives way to further division of power, culminating in the holy democracy where power goes to the people!

But Chinese history went the other way around, showing that there's no historical imperative showing that power must be dissolved more and more as society progresses. The Qing dynasty was larger, stronger, richer and better governed than any previous one. Yet the Emperor had personal rule of all courtly decisions, and even his brothers had to refer to themselves as "slave" in his presence.

Chinese Bureaucracy, 2

2014-01-09

So in talking about how all states end up surrendering real power to the permanent bureaucracy, I thought it interesting to look at the example of China, which has the oldest and most well structured permanent bureaucracy of all. The previous post was on how the Chinese Empire started as a mostly hands-off affair where the Emperors let most daily decisions of government to their ministers, but little by little they assumed more power, until by the Ming Dynasty they assumed personal rule.

Next clip is about the lower levels of government. Who got to be a bureaucrat?[24]

In Ancient China, if you wanted to enter the state bureaucracy, well at the beginning it was all hereditary succession. Which in common parlance means, dragon breeds dragon, phoenix breeds phoenix, and the children of rats dig holes. So that's how it was, the position was inherited every generation. The ruler was like that, and all officials were also like that. Get to the Spring and Autumn

---

[24] https://www.youtube.com/watch?v=gl4ryLN8PyE

period, especially in the Qin state, they had this incentive system to motivate the commoners. If you tilled your land well, you could become an official. At war, those who killed more people could become officials. Those who cut the head of an enemy in the battlefield, would rise one level in the bureaucracy by every head they cut. One head, one level up. Another head, another level up. So why was Qin so strong at war? Well if you're fighting the Qin, your head to them isn't a head. Cut one head, rise one level. And a level means, better salary, housing, land, livestock, wife and children. All yours. So they'll go after you to get that head.

The Qin awarded performance in the battlefield, and unified the country. Yet their empire lasted 15 years, 2 generations. So the Han Dynasty had to rethink how to rule. To beat a country isn't the same as to rule a country, you can't just rely on violence. During war you can rely on blood-minded warriors, but to rule a country you need scholars. But how do I know which scholar is good and which is no good? You need a system to guarantee the quality of the officials. How to do so? Well, local elections. Officials in the provinces would look for good people and promote them to the bureaucracy.

What did they look for exactly? First they looked for talent. And second they looked for morals, if you were filial and frugal. Now given that this relied on people suggesting people, well there's potential for fraud. Talent can be more or less objectively measured. But morals? How do you know if I'm filial and frugal? If I'm not a bureaucrat I'm pretty much forced to be frugal, what am I gonna be corrupt with? And filial virtue is even harder to measure. How do you know if I'm filial? You're gonna come to my house to inspect? See how I kneel on the ground and wash my father's feet? Oh, good kid, very filial. You can't see the bruise dad got after I kicked him yesterday though.

So all this was very hard to measure, and as a result, all this suggestion method, in the end, all those promoted up ended being the children of the higher officials. Not rich people, but high levels of the bureaucracy. Yuan Shao had 3 ministers in 4 generations. Was it hereditary? No, that system was abolished. So how could they have 3 counts in 4 ministers? Well they kept promoting people of their family. Grandpa Yuan An was Chancellor, controlled all the levels of power, had disciples all around the empire. So when promoting someone, who dares not to promote Great Yuan's son?

Later during the Wei-Jin period, it got even worse. In that time all those promoted were from the great families. The biggest were the 4 Big Families: Wang, Xie, Yuan, Xiao, grabbed the levels of power in all Southern Dynasties. In the North they were the Cui, Lu, Li, Zheng, grabbing all power. Not even the Emperor could rival them.

So the Sui Dynasty's Yang Jian, he was a Yang, not a member of the Great Families. So he changed the whole system. This choosing officials by birthright is thing no good. So he set the fairest system of all: an exam. Everybody's equal before the score numbers. This was the start of the Chinese system which lasted 1300 years, the Imperial Examination.

Everybody's equal before the score numbers. Did people cheat? Yes. But without the exam, everybody is cheating. There's no fairness at all. People did cheat at the exams, but the methods of cheating were much less sophisticated than what people use today to cheat in exams. Say, some people would fit a small scroll inside their clothes. So the Court had a good idea, before the exam you all get naked and change into this Exam clothes. But the scholars thought it humiliating. "It's not like each of us is going to cheat, you can't just assume we're all criminals." So what did they do? The Court thought a good one. They set that before the exam, everyone had to go pray to Confucius. And surely before going to pray to the Great Sage, you obviously should bathe, and show your earnestness. So before going to the exam hall, they'd go to the public bath. Then officials would search through your clothes, look for any hidden paper. Once they stopped searching, they'd order the water to stop. Then they'd all come back and wear their clothes again. No humiliation now, huh? Bathing is good, right? If you're poor, you get a free bath, you should be happy.

So there were many ways of preventing cheating. During the Song Dynasty, they hid the names in each exam. Like they do today when they send this closed envelopes. And they not only hid the names, they copied the exams! The examiners never saw the actual handwriting on any exam. A whole group of officials were in charged of copying by hand every exam, 10 exams per official. So the exams that the examiners see all have the same handwriting. The purpose of course is to avoid examiners promoting their own students. They know their students' handwriting, they taught them.

There were lots of these sort of tricks. So under those circumstances, of course some incidents of cheating happened, but it was very hard. There's one example, Qin Hui calls the chief examiner to his house. The examiner dares not refuse the call of the Chancellor, so goes. Once he gets there, the old man is busy so the examiner waits in the library. He waits and waits, and gets very bored. Thing is there are no books on the room, what kind of library is that? So he looks all around trying to find some amusement. All he can see is a piece of paper on top of the table. Being a scholar he's used to reading things, and being bored he's compulsively drawn to the paper. So he grabs the paper, and sees there's a piece of text on it. So he reads it once. The old man still doesn't come. So he reads it again. The old man still doesn't come, so he reads it a third time. And so on until he almost quite memorized the whole thing, he's read it so many time he can recite it backwards. After several hours of wait, a relative of Qin Hui comes, and apologizes: "The Chancellor has been summoned by the Emperor, he won't be able to see you today, please go home." The examiner didn't think twice about it, yeah well Chancellors are busy people, so he goes home.

Days later the Imperial Examination is going on, so they pick up the exams, all those standardized copied exams, and they read him. Then he gets one exam, and huh? "This text is exactly the same as that piece of paper I read on the Chancellors house!" Now see how smart the Chief Examiner is. It's not easy to get to be Chief Examiner. So he understood, "so that's why the Chancellor had me waiting all that day in his library and forced me to read this text. OK then, we got a winner then." Then he opened the envelope with the name, and there it is, Qin Hui's grandson.

So see, the great evil minister Qin Hui, who could kill Yue Fei, betray his country, when it came to the Imperial Examination, he had to go through all this trouble to influence the Chief Examiner. He was afraid the Chief Examiner might not buy the whole thing, and if he hadn't bought it, there's nothing Qin Hui could have done about it. Sure he could have dealt with the Examiner himself, but he had no way of declaring the exam void and making his grandson win. That's we say this system was, relatively speaking, quite fair.

The examination system itself was alright, it was very fair in those times. The problem lied in what questions are asked. In the Song Dynasty the exams were about policy. See how Wen Tianxiang exams have remained to this day, mountains of words criticizing imperial policy. Then came Zhu Yuanzhang, whose culture was rather limited. If the applicants wrote too well he might not understand it, he couldn't read that many letters anyway. So what he did was limit severely what entered the exam. Only the classic books, and only the interpretation of Zhu Xi. That way it's easy to posit the questions, the exam gets easier; it fossilized people's thought.

So over time, people stopped taking the exam seriously. Some examiners just decided the winners by looking at the handwriting. You write nicely, you win. Your handwriting sucks, you're out. The famous Kang Youwei, when he was Liang Qichao's teacher, he was a Xiucai [Level1], while Liang Qichao was a Juren[Level2]. At his age he wasn't even a Juren. Why? Because he had bad handwriting.

So how did he become a Juren later? This is probably legend, but they say the Chief Examiner got his exam, and his first reaction was "what the hell is this crap" and he threw it away. Then he went to the toilet. There was nobody else in the room. Then a servant came in to pour some tea, and he found a scroll in the floor. The servant can't even read, so what did he know. He got the scroll, opened it, put a paperweight on it, and left. After the servant's gone, the examiner comes back from the toilet, not seeing the servant. So he comes into the room and "Huh? I threw away this scroll... How come it's on my desk, and even with a paperweight on it? This must be some heavenly sign, let's take a look then. So he reads the paper, and wow, great piece, exam passed. So Kang Youwei's title of Juren came through the piss of the examiner. They say that after Kang Youwei became famous all he did was give away scrolls of his writing to anyone, just to screw them with his bad handwriting.

So later when people started to reconsider the Imperial Examination, the issue wasn't much the system itself, but what's the content of the exam. Originally you needed deep wisdom of things ancient and new. Then it changed into cherry picking pieces from a handful of books. During the more than 1000 yours that the Examinations went on, the cultural level of the officialdom was extremely high. Including the Emperor, all had to be cultivated. If you aren't well read, and it slips at Court, the ministers will laugh at you. Obviously this doesn't mean all Emperors were of very high culture. There were plenty of thuggish, awful emperors. Especially in the Ming.

Chinese Monarchy

2014-01-13

I started this series with the lecture on Chancellors, and followed with bureaucrats, because I thought it interesting to show how different the dynamics in China were from the West. China is *the* monarchy, they've had deified supreme emperors ruling over tens and hundreds of millions for millennia. Compared to that the monarchies of Europe are pretty much a sham. The Roman Emperors kept their pretenses of being Republican officers for centuries, until the Empire wasn't even in Rome and didn't even speak Latin. Later Medieval and Modern monarchs all had to constantly fight and appease their nobles, only to get their head axed, and those fortunate enough to win that battle would soon lose power to the bourgeoisie.

And that's another funny one, municipal corporations with autonomy rights against the court. The first Chinese to study European history must have scratched their head hard about that. Nothing of the sort ever existed in China. Nobles weren't much of a problem even back in the First Empire, and when the Han Dynasty founder, Liu Bang did give noble rights to his brothers, it didn't take much for his successors to kill them all[25] and stop the experiment. And so the landholding nobility was never an important political force. The absolute power of the monarch was never in question.

Which doesn't mean there weren't any politics, despise Moldbug. The political tensions in Chinese history are mostly those inside the Court, that is, the soap opera-ish fights between the Imperial Family, the eunuchs, bureaucrats, generals, empresses, concubines, male relatives of the concubines, etc. There was enough debate, intrigue, backstabbing to make present parliamentary politics really boring in comparison.

But what were the emperors doing all this time? Let's see Yuan's lecture. This episode isn't that good but I might as well do it first to get to the latter ones.[26]

Today we're gonna talk about: Being Emperor ain't easy.

These days, many compatriots take their history knowledge from TV series. But these TV series aren't always accurate. Now a lot of people enjoy these, especially those majestic scenes with the emperor

---

[25] https://en.wikipedia.org/wiki/Rebellion_of_the_Seven_States

[26] https://www.youtube.com/watch?v=Xex3znGzmJ0&list=PLJ5jfSx82bkHwKohrLzDC00k1-a0AfuVM

reviewing his ministers. You can tell very easily if an actor has played an emperor or not. Those who have get this awesome feeling, everybody kowtowing at them. But was being an emperor so nice really?

Being an emperor ain't easy. Since the First Emperor of Qin established that the emperor was the empire, well being the empire means that you 1 guy has to do everything. You think that's an easy job? It's extremely tiring. Without to mention those farther back, let's just see the Qing emperors.

The Qing emperors had a very strict ritual for all they did. First, they woke up at 4 AM. So what if you don't wake up? Hell I wanna sleep more, I'm feeling lazy today. What if I don't wake up? You get an eunuch at your door yelling "The sun will soon rise, there is much to manage". And you can't just get out and punch the fucker. Yelling is his right given by your ancestors. He'll go on yelling until you wake up.

So the Emperor wakes up, bathes, gets dressed, what then? Breakfast? Nope, who's hungry at that time? So it's reading time. The Emperor wakes up and studies. Kids today complain, Dad goes to work at 8, so he leaves me at school at 6 to study. Well the Emperors did that. The Emperors read first thing in the morning, and spent 2 hours. Reading what? What did the Qing emperors read about? The notes and stories of their ancestors.

Say, the Kangxi emperor. He has to read the stories of his ancestors, but he didn't have that many. His father Shunzhi, died after 18 years of rule. He may have not spoken that much. But imagine the Yongzheng emperor. Then you're screwed. His father ruled for 61 years. All he said every day, all the issues he dealt with. What about Qianlong? His father Yongzheng was a professional emperor. Yongzheng was the most hard working emperor in the history of China. The craziest emperor of them all. How crazy? Every year, he would only rest the day of his birthday. In 13 years of rule, he left 18,000,000 characters [divide per 3 and you get a rough equivalent in english words] of handwritten records. Do the math, more than a million characters per year. More than me and I write best-selling books. And I'm a speaker, I speak and other write down and edit what I spoke. But the Yongzheng emperor was writing. 3-4k characters every day. A normal guy typing 4k characters on a PC gets tired. The Emperor wrote 3-4k with a brush!

You think the Emperor had time every day to think about this or that concubine? He didn't have time for that. So when you look at the Qing palace and look at all those Travel Records of the Yongzheng emperor, pictures of him fishing, hunting, travelling, why did he had all those pictures made? He really envied that sort of life. He couldn't do all that. So he got tired, got himself some Daoist potion of eternal life, and died of mercury oxide poisoning.

See? Being an Emperor ain't easy. 4 AM wake up, then 7 AM there's morning court session. Meet all military ministers, or any official he wants to talk to. At 9 AM he eats breakfast, 2 PM he has lunch, and that's it, 2 meals a day. He might get some small bites at night. Every day of an emperor is full of stress, with little time for himself. The Emperor is seldom in his quarters, let alone going out and picking up the ladies. No way. The arrangements were very strict. Everything he did in a day was documented, every word he said was recorded by special bureaucrats.

And say the Emperor says something not very suitable and wants the recorded to omit it. Well he didn't have that power. Every single word had to be recorded truthfully, to transmit to his descendents, so when his descendents take the throne, they can see how he handled things, step by step. So an Emperor's day was always very busy.

In TV shows you can always see the characters talking about "going to court". Now, going to court wasn't a constant thing. In the Qing era there was court every 10 days. The Emperor didn't go to court every day. And where was this court thing? Not inside the palace. Everybody's been to the Forbidden City, the Hall of Supreme Harmony isn't that big, is it? All the ministers didn't fit up there.

So what'd they do? In the Qing era, the Emperor presided over the court on the Gates of Heavenly Purity, outside.

The Emperor sat down on the gate, the ministers at the square. So imagine a 35º sauna day. Why did they have court at 7 AM in the morning? Well they'd all die if they did it at noon. They'd boil in their own sweat. So Morning Court was cool in summer, but what about winter? 7 AM in the morning, -30º cold, those days there was no urban heat island thing, no global warming, so it was freezing.

So what'd they do? Just do it. The Emperor had lots of layers of clothes, nice leather coats with fur and stuff, and the ministers had to stay there and listen too. Bureaucrats in old China didn't have expense accounts. They had to buy their own housing, all expenses had to be paid from their own pockets, including court attire. Nobody gave them to you. If you got money, you wore fur, if you didn't have money, you wore cotton, if you couldn't afford cotton we'll you're screwed. Anyway the Emperor had all those nice fox tails on him, and you had to be there too in court.

Usually it was 1 court every 10 days, but in the time of Kangxi, Yongzheng and Qianlong, especially with Kangxi and Qianlong, they had court almost every day. I guess that their ministers didn't have it easy either. Court every day, busy as hell. Being Emperor was really hard work, nothing awesome or romantic like those TV shows, with the Emperor constantly flirting with the concubines. Where there Emperors who did that? Well yeah. But those lewd Emperors in Chinese histories all had really bad endings. Chinese history has both tyrants and lousy emperors. The tyrants weren't incompetent, they were quite capable, but used their ability to do bad things. But they did take care of government. Lousy emperors didn't. Liu Bei's son is the most typical one.

Chinese Monarchy, 2

2014-01-16 // china, history, monarchy, bureaucracy, series

So we've seen that in the eternal conflict between the Chinese Emperor and his Bureaucracy, slowly the Emperor took power from the bureaucrats and into his own hands. As a result the Emperors ended up being extremely busy, having to handle all imperial business by themselves.

But the Chinese Emperors had quite extensive harems, and many of them sired dozens of children. All of which was necessary for the continuity of the dynasty of course. So what happened with all those Imperial Princes? Did the Monarch use his family to control the bureaucrats? Did he enlist their help to run the business of government? Let's see Yuan Tengfei's take on the issue:

I translate 王 as prince, following common practice. For more details see Wikipedia[27].

Princes are Miserable[28]

---

[27] https://en.wikipedia.org/wiki/Chinese_nobility#After_Zhou_Dynasty

In Ancient China, the Emperor is boss. So the princes must be second in command. In today's soap operas, it's sorta the same way. If an actor can't get to play an emperor, well he can get to play a prince and enjoy it. All those Imperial Princes, very cool.

But being a Prince was actually quite miserable. First I must correct an idea that most people have. Who get to be prince? In my classes I always asked my students: who gets to receive the title of Prince? And they always say: "the Emperor's relatives". Wrong. His uncle-in law can? His sister's son? No. They have to be from the inner family. That is, the same surname. Brother, uncle, son, brother's son, paternal cousin, can be princes.

So after you get the title of Prince, you get an awesome life, right? There's an old saying in China: those unfortunate born at the imperial family. That's not being contrarian, that's not faking it, not the words of a rich fuck who's bored of eating seafood ad envies the simple food of the peasant. No, the author really meant it. Why?

Everybody knows, when the First Emperor of Qin unified China, he wondered: why did the realm of the Zhou kings fall into disorder? Because he gave fiefs to all those nobles. I won't do that, I'll set provinces and commanderies, and I'll be the boss. I say the orders, and they'll go top-down I

---

[28] https://www.youtube.com/watch?v=Do_rnR09T_c

control the Chancellor, the Chancellor controls the governor, the governor controls the province chief the province chief controls village heads, everything top-down, my imperial policies will be implemented directly. Awesome idea.

As a result, the First Emperor was too too good, but his son was no good, so the empire collapsed in 15 years. Then Liu Bang grabbed power. Liu Bang had no culture at all, born a country thug. Well he grabbed power and needed a conclusion: why did the Qing fall in 15 years? Liu Bang during the Qin Dynasty was a neighborhood patrol officer, running around with a small team walking around the streets. When the Emperor came out of the palace, he'll be ordered to keep peace, making people shout welcome and all that. That's what he was doing. So when he has to come up with the reason the Qin Empire fell, well he couldn't make a very fine analysis. So he got the wrong conclusion. He thought that it was precisely because the Qin Emperor had not given fiefs to his male relatives, so when the time came and people wanted to overthrew him, his brothers didn't have armies, so they couldn't go rescue him.

That's why Liu Bang gave big fiefs to all his family. He made princes of all his sons and nephews, to protect him. "You're of my own blood, you can't go against me!" Well no, they won't go against you. But once you're dead, well then it's a different story. What when your son gets the throne? Just when the Emperor Wen got the throne, all these princes started to get upity. When the Emperor Jing got the throne, Liu Piu, prince of Wu rebelled. Liu Pi saw the Emperor and just didn't like him. Why the fuck do you get to be Emperor, huh? I'm your elder uncle. And yes, Liu Pi surely was Liu Qi (Emperor Jing)'s uncle. I didn't get to be Emperor, why the hell would you? If you can be Emperor, so can I. So he rebelled, joined by a bunch of brothers and uncles, the Seven State Rebellion, causing great havoc to the dynasty.

After the rebellion was over, the Emperor thought: everybody wants to sit on this chair I have my ass on. But who is the biggest threat? The Emperor thought. My uncles. My brothers. My nephews. Even my sons! Why are they the biggest threat? Well as I said, because they are all Liu. My surname's Yuan, if I took the throne, that would be usurpation. Yuan Shu wanted to grab the throne, then Cao Cao rose against him and he was fucked. But hey, if I'm Liu, family of the Emperor, if he gets the throne I can have it too. If we talk about the bloodline I've an even closer relative to the previous Emperor!

So from the Han Dynasty onwards, the biggest object of concern of the Emperors were all these uncles. The Emperor had to control all these paternal relatives. What to do? From the Han Dynasty onwards, they established a principle: titles without fiefs. The old Zhou Dynasty had this feudalism system, with princes and their fiefs. Starting with the Han Dynasty, the nobles had titles but no fiefs. I name you the Prince of Qi, but don't get uppity now. You have no power over the land of Qi, at most you're a big landlord over there, with some land and money. But you'll have no say over the administration or the military in Qi.

Fast forward to the Ming and Qing dynasties, they got this new idea. Giving country names to Princes makes it easy for them to get vain. If I name a Prince of Qi then he gest this idea the land of Qi is his. What if he rebels? So starting in the late Ming era, all through the Qing, prince titles stopped using country or dynasty names. They started using fancy names. The Prince of Happiness, Prince of Reverence, Prince of Courtesy, etc. So princes now stopped using country names, lest they got the wrong idea.

So yeah you're a Prince, but you have no real power. If you have a title of Prince, but no real job in the court, well you're just some big landlord. And your life isn't as nice and leisurely as that of a normal landlord. Why? Because this Emperor relative of yours is constantly watching you. In Beijing there's several tombs of the Han era. They found them recently, and TV went on to broadcast the whole thing, but they had to stop at the middle. No way to show that on TV. Why? There was nothing inside it, not even the gravestone, all stolen. People suspect that in one of these tombs there's the body of Liu Dan, Prince of Yan.

How did he die? The Annals of History say that during the celebrations of Spring, he showed the appearance of an Emperor. That's all. The guy was in Beijing, far away from the Emperor in Xi'An. So he thought hey the mountains are high, the emperor is far away, I'll just show off a bit, he'll never know. Just that. Ok. The princedom Chancellor, who was there sent by the Emperor to watch on the Prince, sent a text to the Emperor, "this Liu Dan kid is getting uppity, see this pic as proof", and sent an MMS to the Emperor. Immediately a courier rode from Chang An with a small bottle of poison, commanding Liu Dan to kill himself. And he just had this moment of vanity, he hadn't rebelled. So Liu Dan had to kill himself, but his son got to inherit his title. But had he rebelled? Oh that's fucked. His whole family would be wiped out from the face of the earth.

During the Ming Dynasty, all Princes were forbidden from staying in Beijing. Once they got named Princes, they had to beat it, quick, can't stay in Beijing. And once you reached your destination, it wasn't that different from being in prison. Can't move 20km from your palace. Wanna go hunting? OK, can't move further than 20 km from the city. Bureaucrats will protect you. Well they say they will protect you, you know what they're actually doing. Every day they come visit to drink tea with ya. Any new kids in the family? How are your household goods? Anything missing? Something new? A new blade perhaps? Got a spear hiding somewhere? Some gunpowder?

You're an Imperial Prince, but your mother didn't come with you. Your mother is an imperial concubine. So the Imperial concubine dies in Beijing, your mother died. You wanna go to Beijing and attend the funeral. No fucking way, don't even think about it. Asking your Emperor brother or uncle is like asking to be killed. Unless, there's one chance, the Emperor is your full brother. Same mother. Or if your relation with the Emperor is really good. Then he might allow you to go to the capital and pay your respects. But during the Ming Dynasty, the rule was that to pay your respects in Beijing you could only get up to Lugou Bridge (the outter limit of the city). It's not like you can enter Beijing, get into the Forbidden City and attend the funeral. No way. Wanna get around the body? Nope. All you can do is go to Lugou bridge, cry looking at the capital, and get the fuck out. Yeah yeah your voice is big enough, your mother heard you, now out.

The Qing Dynasty was the exact opposite of the Ming. The Ming forced the princes out of the capital, the Qing Dynasty forced them to stay in Beijing. If you see today in Beijing there's lots of prince palaces, and that's because they couldn't leave the city. The Qing Dynasty had much fewer princes than the Ming, so they kept them in the capital. Unless you had a job in the administration, a simple Prince in the Qing dynasty could not go out of the second ring road. Can't get out, if you leave your cousin the Emperor will miss you so much. So stay in your small city please. So these people cried, those unfortunate born at the imperial family.

So no Aristocracy in China. The Imperial Princes of China are quite lucky compared to those of the Turkish House of Osman, who were subject to a ritual game of Battle Royale and killed each other until only one was left. Monarchy is a high-stakes game, and high-stakes games get nasty very fast. Especially when the institution of the Harem more or less guarantees Elite Overproduction of the worst sort.

European royalty didn't suffer of same problem because enforced monogamy barely produced enough heirs to maintain the dynasty. Which produced a different, perhaps even worse result: international wars of succession, a distinctly European phenomenon.

In Chinese history, the aim of strengthening the power of the Emperor was focused mostly on dismantling the nobility, which was achieved by developing a permanent bureaucracy in its place.

210 - Historic China

WMLC Pamphlets

Defenses	Bonald
Singularities	Jim
Writings of the Inquisitor	Jim
Asia	Spandrell
Bioleninism	Spandrell
Historic China	Spandrell
Modern China	Spandrell
First Week Actions	Donald J. Trump
First Week Remarks	Donald J. Trump

212 - Historic China